I Shrank My Teacher

DON'T MISS THE REST OF THE
SIXTH-GRADE ALIENS SERIES!

SIXTH-GRADE ALIEN

I Shrank My Teacher

Previously titled
The Attach of the Two-Inch Teacher

by **BRUCE COVILLE**

Illustrated by Glen Mullaly

ALADDIN
NEW YORK   LONDON   TORONTO   SYDNEY   NEW DELHI

ALADDIN

An imprint of Simon & Schuster Children's Publishing Division

1230 Avenue of the Americas, New York, New York 10020

This Aladdin hardcover edition August 2020

Text copyright © 1999, 2020 by Bruce Coville

Previously published in 1999 as *The Attack of the Two-Inch Teacher*

Illustrations copyright © 2020 by Glen Mullaly

Also available in an Aladdin paperback edition.

All rights reserved, including the right of reproduction in whole or in part in any form.

ALADDIN and related logo are registered trademarks of Simon & Schuster, Inc.

For information about special discounts for bulk purchases, please contact Simon & Schuster Special Sales at 1-866-506-1949 or business@simonandschuster.com.

The Simon & Schuster Speakers Bureau can bring authors to your live event. For more information or to book an event contact the Simon & Schuster Speakers Bureau at 1-866-248-3049 or visit our website at www.simonspeakers.com.

Book designed by Tiara Iandiorio

The illustrations for this book were rendered in in a mix of traditional and digital media.

The text of this book was set in Noyh Book.

Manufactured in the United States of America 0620 BVG

2 4 6 8 10 9 7 5 3 1

Library of Congress Control Number 2020935834

This book has been cataloged with the Library of Congress.

ISBN 9781534464803 (hc)

ISBN 9781534464797 (pbk)

ISBN 9781534464810 (eBook)

CONTENTS

TO VENETIA GOSLING,
MY CHAMPION IN THE
UNITED KINGDOM

I Shrank My Teacher

CHAPTER 1

[PLESKIT]
A LETTER HOME

FROM: Pleskit Meenom, on the deeply weird Planet Earth
TO: Maktel Geebrit, on my beloved Planet Hevi-Hevi

Dear Maktel:

After my first week on Earth, I thought things might settle down a little.

Guess what? The next two weeks were just as difficult. What makes it even worse is that while the problems the first week were not my fault, this time the whole mess happened because I did something stupid. *Really* stupid.

1

Why do things always get so out of control for me? I sure didn't mean to shrink Ms.
Weintraub. I wouldn't even have brought the
Molecule Compactor to school if I hadn't
been so desperate and angry.

But I'm getting ahead of myself.

The whole mess started because my new
friend Tim decided we should try to get me
to be a little more "cool."

I know the translator is going to have a problem with this word cool because it is not like
anything we have on Hevi-Hevi. As near as I
can figure out, it has to do with getting people
to like you because you are (a) different and (b)
just like them. If you think this is confusing, just
be glad you don't have to try to be cool yourself. It's very tiring. Except Linnsy, my other
new friend, says it doesn't work to try being
cool anyway. Either you are, or you aren't.

This being "cool" seems to be one of the
great mysteries of life here. I have not figured
it out yet, but working on it led to my most
recent problem.

I Shrank My Teacher

I've written out the whole story for you. Actually, Tim and I wrote it together, just like last time. You'll find it in the attached files.

Tim is turning out to be a really good friend. But please do not worry; that does not mean you are not still my friend, too. I hope you can visit soon! Even if this planet is strange and scary, it can be kind of fun.

Until then—*Fremmix Bleeblom!*

Your pal,

Pleskit

CHAPTER 2

[TIM]
OFF TO THE EMBASSY

"Hey, Tim. This is Pleskit. Do you want to come over and share activities?"

Getting an invitation to a friend's house might not seem like a big deal to you. But when that friend is the first alien kid to go to school openly on Earth, I think it's pretty exciting.

"Just a minute," I replied. "I have to ask my mom."

This was pretty much a formality. I knew Mom would say yes—mostly because I also knew that if she didn't my brain would explode, and I figured she didn't want that to happen.

To my surprise, getting permission wasn't as simple

as I had expected. My mother wrinkled her brow and said, "I don't know, Tim. It might be dangerous over there."

"For Pete's sake, Mom! The embassy could survive a bomb blast. Pleskit even has his own personal body-guard."

"Which proves my point! Why would he have a bodyguard if there isn't any danger? And his so-called bodyguard didn't stop that evil hamster-woman alien from trying to empty your brains last night. She's still on the loose."

"Mikta-makta-mookta has probably left the planet by now. Besides, this is a matter of national security. If I don't go, Pleskit might take it as an insult! Do you want to offend the son of the first ambassador from outer space? We might cause an interplanetary incident!"

Mom sighed. "Sometimes I worry that you're going to grow up to be a lawyer, Tim. All right, you can go. But I expect you home for supper!"

That was fine with me. I may be interested in all things alien, but after my first experience with Hevi-Hevian food I was ready to let my stomach rest for a while.

I ran back to the phone. "I'll be right over!"

"Do you want me to send Ralph to get you?"

"Nah, I'll ride my bike."

"That sounds nice," said Pleskit wistfully.

I felt kind of sorry for him. Pleskit has to travel in a big limousine, driven by a guy named Ralph. It's kind of cool the first couple of times you ride in it. And it's a lot nicer than my mother's beat-up old Pontiac. But having to ride in it *everywhere* makes it kind of like a very fancy prison.

I can see the alien embassy from our apartment. Actually, you can see it from a lot of places in town, since it is built on top of a hill in Thorncraft Park and is very big. It's also very weird. Basically, it looks like a flying saucer suspended from a big hook that curves up from the ground. (The hook is sort of like the top part of a coat hanger, except it's a couple of hundred feet high.)

As usual, a big crowd was gathered at the edge of the force field that marks the embassy grounds, gawking up at the saucer. There were only a few protesters now, but their anti-alien signs were pretty rude. Mostly people were taking pictures and stuff. I saw on the news that hotel rooms are sold out for fifty miles around Syracuse because of people wanting to see the aliens. I felt very privileged to be allowed in.

The first time I had entered the embassy I was in the limo with Pleskit and we went in by way of a tunnel that opens a fair distance from the hook. This time I got off my bike and pushed my way through the crowd until I reached a small blue dome that stands about fifty yards from the base of the embassy, right at the edge of the force field. I knocked on the door. The guy inside frowned at me. Then he looked at the control panel in front of him, looked at me again, and switched on a microphone.

"Place your hand against the wall," he said.

I did as he instructed. My palm tingled for a moment.

The guard nodded. "You pass." He pressed another button, and a panel slid up in front of me. I could hear murmurs of jealousy from the crowd as I wheeled my bike inside the dome.

The guard, who was a human, held up a hand and said, "Greetings, Earthling." Then he cracked up, as if this was some brilliant joke.

I thought about answering, "Greetings, Bone-head!" but decided against it.

I leaned my bike against the wall, then climbed into a silver-and-crimson capsule. It was about the size of my teacher's desk. The seat was padded, and as soon as I sat down, it shifted to fit my butt.

The guard closed the top over me. It was clear, so I could see right through it.

The capsule slid forward into a silver-sided tunnel. The top went dark. Weird alien music began to play around me. At least, I assumed it was music; a bunch of high, tinkly sounds with a windlike noise behind them. The music couldn't have been playing for more than ten seconds when the top of the capsule turned clear again.

I thought something must have gone wrong until I glanced to my right and saw a familiar purple face smiling at me.

"Greetings, Earthling!" said Pleskit. His *sphen-gnut-ksher* (that's the knob that grows out of the top of his bald head) bent forward, as if taking a tiny bow.

I was totally startled. "How did I get here so fast?" I glanced down at the capsule I was sitting in. "Is this a matter transmitter or something?" I wondered nervously if my molecules had been dissembled and put back together.

Pleskit laughed. "We wouldn't use a matter transmitter for a short trip like that!" (I figured this must mean they actually *have* matter transmitters.)

"But I didn't even know I was moving!"

"Now you can see why I don't like riding in that limousine! Come on—let's go do something."

As I was climbing out of the capsule, something poked its head over Pleskit's shoulder.

I jumped back in alarm. "What's *that?*"

CHAPTER 3

[PLESKIT]
LANGUAGE TALK

Tim seemed extremely startled to see my Veeblax peeking over my shoulder. Then I realized that he had not met the little creature before.

The Veeblax was in its resting form, which makes it look something like what Earthlings call a lizard, though its colors are much brighter. Also, it was trying out three different tails at the moment. Tim's shout of alarm caused it to transform itself into a lump the same color as my garment. This was not an extremely effective way to hide. But the Veeblax is young, and still learning.

"This is my pet," I said. I stroked the Veeblax

reassuringly. It cooed, raised one eye on a stalk, and cautiously began to examine Tim.

"That's cool!" said Tim.

This was the first time I noticed him using the word that was to turn out to be such a problem for me, and I misunderstood. "The Veeblax is not really cool," I said. "In fact, it's quite warm. Do you want to touch it?"

Tim smiled. *"Cool* just means something is neat. And I'd love to touch it."

I shook my head. "Alas, the Veeblax is not neat, either. The messes it creates are one of the main reasons the Fatherly One is not entirely happy that I have it."

Looking a bit nervous, Tim reached out to touch my little shape-shifter. "That's still not what I mean," he said, speaking softly now. *"Cool* and *neat* both mean something is . . . groovy."

"Ah! Well, the Veeblax *can* be groovy, though at the moment it is totally smooth."

Tim rolled his eyes. "Groovy means . . . oh, never mind. Can I hold it?"

"That is all right with me," I said, feeling a little unhappy about this fuss we were having over words. "Put out your hands and see if it will come to you."

Tim did as I said, but the Veeblax clung to my shoulder. Possibly it was picking up on my negative feelings. "Never mind," I said. "It just needs a while to get used to you."

"Just like everyone else," said Tim glumly.

My negative feelings grew stronger. "Tim, look who you are talking to! Do you expect *me*, the only purple kid on the planet, to feel sympathy because people have trouble getting used to *you?*"

Tim laughed. "You've got a point."

At the sound of his laugh the Veeblax poked out another eyestalk.

Relaxing a little, I said, "Let's go see if Shhh-foop has anything we can eat."

"I'm not all that hungry," replied Tim quickly. He sounded a little nervous. This dismayed me, for the sharing of food is a basic way of bonding on almost all planets.

"Gleep!" said the Veeblax. "Gleep! Gleep!"

"Well, you may not be hungry," I said. "But the Veeblax is. Come on, I have to get him a snack."

My bodyguard, Robert McNally, was already sitting in the kitchen. McNally (that is what he likes to be called) is a tall, powerful man with dark brown skin. He lives in the embassy with us. But because the building itself is well guarded, he is only officially on duty when I have to go somewhere.

The Fatherly One's slimeball assistant Barvgis was sitting with McNally. When I call Barvgis a slimeball, I do not mean it in a bad way, as Earthlings seem to. It is simply a description. Barvgis is quite round, and his skin is slimy. So he is a slimeball.

At the moment he was a gloomy-looking slimeball. This was unusual for him, as he is normally quite cheerful.

Shhh-foop, who does our cooking, was bringing McNally a cup of coffee. Tim and I stopped to watch.

"Ooodlie-opp, snipple geeblies," she sang happily as she used one of the orange tentacles growing from her head to set the cup in front of him. "I think we have it this time, Mr. McNally!"

McNally looked at Shhh-foop nervously, then raised the cup to his lips. He sniffed the black liquid, blew across its surface, then took a small sip. Instantly his face puckered into a very unusual expression. Setting the cup down, he whispered hoarsely, "Not quite, Shhh-foop."

Barvgis chuckled. But Shhh-foop's tentacles drooped, and she moved very slowly as she slid back to the counter, warbling, "O caffeine bean, O caffeine bean, why will you not do as I wish and make the coffee for which McNally longs?"

"Hey, it's the dynamic duo," said McNally, noticing

I Shrank My Teacher

Tim and me for the first time. "Ready for another day of thrills and adventure?"

"No!" I said earnestly. "I had enough thrills yesterday."

McNally laughed. "Chill, Pleskit. I was just kidding."

"What is this thing with Earthlings and coldness? First Tim wants me to be cool. Now you tell me to chill. I do not understand. I am comfortable at my current temperature!"

McNally looked startled. But before he could speak, Tim said, "I've got a question."

"What is it?" I asked. I set the Veeblax on the table, where it began trying to imitate McNally's coffee cup.

Tim looked uncomfortable. "Well, this confusion we keep having over *cool* got me wondering about language. The thing is, you speak our language really well. You don't have an accent or anything. Heck, sometimes I think you know more words than I do—you sure use more big words when you talk. But every once in a while you get screwed up by a word that seems totally simple to me. So I was just wondering how you learned and stuff."

Before I could answer, Shhh-foop came gliding back to the table with a bowl of *splurgis* nuggets. Their savory aroma and twisty green stems sent little love songs to my tongue. Though I was longing to take one, I waited while she extended the bowl to Tim. "Snackie-pie, my little Earthling cutie?" she sang.

"No thanks, Shhh-foop," said Tim. He spoke quickly, and I thought I saw a flash of terror on his face.

Shhh-foop sighed musically, set the bowl on the table, and slid back to her work area.

"You should always try at least a bite of something," said Barvgis softly. "It is one of the first rules of diplomacy."

"Hey, give the kid a break," said McNally. "It hasn't even been a full day since you guys turned his stomach inside out with those *finnikle-pokta* things. And you still haven't answered his question, which is something I've been wondering about myself."

I looked longingly at the *splurgis* nuggets. On Hevi-Hevi we have a rule that the host may not eat before his guest does. But we also have an expectation that the guest will take at least a bite of anything that is served to him. I was not sure if Tim's breaking the rule meant that I could break it, also. Barvgis sighed, and I could tell that he was even more eager to eat some than I was.

I Shrank My Teacher

I decided to answer Tim's question, hoping that the wonderful odor of the nuggets would tempt him to try a taste while I spoke.

"Learning a language is a two-step process for us," I said. "The first part is fairly easy; we take a pill that makes the brain receptive to new language."

"How does it do that?" interrupted Tim.

"It makes the brain temporarily more childlike," said Barvgis. "Little kids learn language at an astonishing rate. So we put the brain in the same chemical state as it is at the time of the 'language explosion.' We take this pill just before going to sleep. Then we put on a helmet, and all through the night the new language is pumped into our brain. Ten nights of this is usually enough to get the basic command of a language."

Tim's eyes were wide. "That's cool!"

"There you go again!" I said. "Things like *cool* we do not learn. I mean, I know the word, but not the way you use it. The program gave me the basics of language. But it is very formal."

"Sounds a little like having a dictionary installed in your head," said McNally.

"Yes!" I said. "But the definitions are very literal. To

play in a language, to be creative with it, that you can only learn by *using* the language. And I have observed that people here play with words a lot. I think many of you are secretly poets—or would be, if you had the chance. But that does make it hard for me to understand you sometimes."

"Well, we'll just have to work on that," said McNally.

He reached for his coffee cup.

Then he began to scream.

CHAPTER 4

[TIM]

WE MEET MS. BUTTSMAN

Pleskit's bodyguard is a tough guy. He packs a gun and I figure he knows all kinds of martial arts and stuff. I'm using him as the hero of a comic book I'm trying to write.

So I was surprised to hear him scream In terror.

On the other hand, I suppose I would have screamed, too, if I had picked up my coffee cup and it turned into a squirming lizard-thing in my hand. I could tell McNally wanted to drop it—mostly because he leaped to his feet and began shouting "Ai! Ai! Ai!" while he shook his arm. But the Veeblax wasn't letting go. It clung to McNally's hand, shrieking "Gleep! Gleep! Gleepitty-gleep-glop!"

"Stop! Stop! Oh, stoppitty-stop-stop!" cried Pleskit, sort of rhyming with the Veeblax. He was on his feet, too, dancing around and wringing his purple hands. "You must stop, Mr. McNally. You are terrifying the poor little creature."

"Terrifying *it!*" shouted McNally, still shaking his arm. "What about *me?*"

"What is going on here?" roared a new voice.

I spun toward the door. Meenom Ventrah, Pleskit's parental unit, stood there looking big, purple, and cranky. Next to him was a female human. She was tall and slender, with pale blond hair that came just past her ears. She was dressed in a dark blue business suit, and her face had kind of a pinched look.

"It's all right, O Fatherly One," said Pleskit, not even turning toward him. "Just a little problem with the Veeblax." Lowering his voice, he said desperately to McNally, "It will let go if you will only *hold still!*"

McNally stopped trying to shake the Veeblax off his hand. I could see him take a deep breath. Stretching out his arm, he lowered his hand gently to the table. The Veeblax was still shrieking and squirming. That was when I decided McNally was pretty heroic after all.

I know *I* couldn't have held still with all that going on at the end of my arm!

Pleskit held up one of the yukky-looking things Shhh-foop had put on the table and began making kissy noises. The Veeblax stopped shrieking. Then it stopped squirming. Next it put out three or four eye-stalks. An instant later it slithered off McNally's hand, scurried across the table, and stood on its hind legs.

"Gleep?" it said hopefully.

Pleskit dropped the nugget of food into the creature's mouth. It swallowed it in one bite. Then, cooing happily, it scrambled up his arm and onto his shoulder.

"Well," said the woman standing next to Meenom. "I see what you mean." Her voice was stiff and cold, as if she had just smelled something nasty.

"Greetings, Fatherly One," said Pleskit. He was stroking the Veeblax, trying to keep it calm.

"Greetings, Pleskit. And good morning to you, Mr. McNally. And you, Timothy."

For a moment I was surprised that such an important person as Meenom would remember me. But I guess remembering people is part of being a good diplomat.

"And you, Shhh-foop," he added as the cook slid into sight, singing modestly to herself.

She waved her tentacles in response.

Meenom gestured to the woman standing next to him. "I want you all to meet Ms. Kathryn Buttsman. She is joining our staff today as protocol officer."

"Protocol officer?" asked McNally.

Meenom nodded. "After the bizarre incidents of the last few days, I realized we needed someone to help us navigate the strange paths of Earthling culture. I sent an urgent request to our host government last night, and they responded by sending us this lady. She has graciously put aside her other projects to join us on an emergency basis. I especially appreciate this as it will be several days before headquarters can send me a replacement for Mikta-makta-mookta."

"It is my pleasure to be of service," said Ms. Buttsman. She smiled broadly. "I will do all I can to guide you to a better understanding of my people." Looking at Pleskit and the Veeblax, she narrowed her eyes. With a smile that could have chilled an iceberg, she added, "I think I can be of special use in helping the young gentleman fit in with the better elements of society."

Uh-oh, I thought.

And I was right.

CHAPTER 5

[PLESKIT]
AIR MATTRESS

As soon as the Fatherly One had led Ms. Buttsman away, McNally made a low whistling sound. "Pleskit, my little purple pal, I think we've got us a problem."

At first I did not understand. "Please, McNally, do not be angry at the Veeblax. It was an honest mistake, and it was frightened."

"It's not the Veeblax I'm talking about, kid. It's the ice queen."

"More coldness!" I cried in frustration. "I do not understand!"

"Cool is good, cold is bad," said Tim.

I Shrank My Teacher

"So it's a matter of degree?" I asked, still confused.

Tim laughed, and I realized that I had accidentally made a joke. My first joke in the language of the Earthlings! This was a good thing. If only I had done it on purpose. . . .

"Let's just say that Ms. Buttsman doesn't look like the warm, fuzzy type," said McNally.

I wondered if I would ever be not confused again. "Why should she be warm and fuzzy? She is a human, not a Grindbullian or something."

McNally sighed. "I just mean that our new staff member does not seem very friendly."

"She's not," said Barvgis gloomily. "That is what I was about to tell you about when Tim and Pleskit arrived. Based on my first conversation with her, I believe she must have eaten a rule book when she was a baby."

McNally started to reach for his coffee cup, then pulled his hand back nervously. "Look, I'll see you guys later. I'll be in my room if you need me."

I decided this was a good time for Tim and me to go to my room, too. So we bid Barvgis farewell and left the kitchen. I believe he was very happy to be left with the rest of the *splurgis* nuggets.

Tim was excited about going to my room. It had not been included in the official tour I gave him, his mother, and Linnsy the night before, so this was going to be the first time he saw it.

"Whoa!" he cried when I touched the pad that causes the door to slide into the wall. "It's so . . . *clean!*"

"Clean is good, is it not?" I asked, leading the way into the room.

"Yeah, I guess so," said Tim uncertainly. "I'm just not really used to it."

This made me curious. "What does your room look like?"

"Like a bomb hit it, according to my mother. But she's a real fussbudget about that kind of thing."

"She budgets her fussing?" I asked in fascination. "Does that mean she only gets to fuss a certain amount each day? Like a fuss allowance? What an interesting concept. I wonder if I could get the Fatherly One to consider such an arrangement!"

Tim laughed. "It's just a saying, Pleskit. It means she fusses a *lot.*"

I sighed. "You have *such* a strange language! It is

bad enough that you make each word have many meanings, as if there were not enough sounds and smells to go around. But then you let the meanings fight with each other!"

"What do you mean?"

"Budget! From what my language programs taught me, one uses a budget to limit how much one spends of something—as in 'I am on a budget.' But now you call your mother a fussbudget because she does so much of it! I do not know if I will ever master this strangeness. Come on. Let's go jump on the bed."

"What bed?" asked Tim. It was his turn to look puzzled. "I don't see a bed at all. I was wondering where you sleep."

"I have an air mattress."

Now Tim looked completely baffled. "You live in this totally cool place, you're from a super-powerful alien race, and you sleep on an air mattress?"

"It's very comfortable," I said, starting to feel annoyed. With my *sphen-gnut-ksher* I emitted the smell of sleepiness. At the same time, I farted the medium fart of summoning. This pair of signals caused the mattress to form itself.

I climbed onto it.

Tim looked at me in astonishment. "How did you do that?"

"Do what? Climb on. It's fun!"

CHAPTER 6

[TIM]
BED BOUNCING

Pleskit looked like he was bouncing on nothing. And with each jump he went higher into the air.
But though he was getting closer and closer to the
ceiling, his feet never touched the floor—never got
more than about ten inches away from it.

I couldn't resist. Stepping forward, I lowered my
hand toward the floor.

Something pressed back up against it.

"What is this?" I asked, delighted, but still a little
nervous.

"I told you," said Pleskit, still bouncing. "It's air!
Actually, it's what we call 'thick air,' controlled and

contained by a molecular shield. Come on, Tim, what are you waiting for?"

Reminding myself that I had wanted strange new experiences, I scrambled up beside him.

It was about the coolest thing ever. The air, wherever it was coming from, had just enough strength to hold us up. If you put pressure against it, it put pressure back. And if you jumped . . . well, the result was BOING-G-G-G-G!

It was like a trampoline where you had taken out the canvas but somehow kept the springiness. I started doing flips and butt bounces. Pleskit did a swan dive. I wanted to try one of those myself, but didn't have the guts to plunge face-first toward the floor when I couldn't see what was going to stop me from hitting it.

Soon we were laughing like a couple of lunatics. I kept expecting someone to come to the door and tell us to stop. But when Pleskit's Fatherly One *did* stick his head in to see what was going on, he just nodded in satisfaction, then went away without saying a word.

"He doesn't mind that we're doing this?" I asked in surprise.

"Why should he?" replied Pleskit, equally surprised.

I Shrank My Teacher

When I thought about it, I couldn't come up with any good reason. I mean, it wasn't like we were going to ruin the mattress or anything.

As we were jumping, I was also checking out Pleskit's room. It was shaped a little like the wide end of a giant piece of pie. That is, the outer wall was slightly curved and the two side walls slanted toward each other. Because the embassy was so big, the slant was hardly noticeable. The fourth wall, the one closest to the center of the embassy, was about twelve feet long. Also, the room had no real corners. The places where the walls met were smoothly rounded.

The outer wall was mostly clear, as if it was made out of glass. (I figured it must actually be some sort of super-space material.) Underneath it ran a shelf covered with all sorts of gadgets. Boy, was I itching to get a chance to find out what those things were!

What I did *not* see were any clothes. This looked pretty odd to me, since I mostly keep my clothes on the floor. Even odder, I didn't see any place where he *could* keep them.

"Hey, Pleskit," I said, landing on my butt and boinging into the air again. "Don't you have a closet or anything?"

"Of course I do," he replied, heading face-first for the floor. The air mattress caught him, of course, and as he was bouncing up again he clapped his hands and farted.

It was a very musical fart—two short notes and a long one. A door slid open in the wall.

"See," said Pleskit. "A closet."

"Did you just . . . uh . . . signal that to open?" I asked. Without intending to, I jumped toward the closet. To my surprise, I landed on the floor with a thud and fell to my butt.

"You should have stayed on the bed," said Pleskit, jumping down to join me. "Is your behind part all right?"

"Yeah, I think so." I got to my feet and rubbed my rear. "They ought to put guardrails on that thing."

"We do not believe in guardrails," replied Pleskit. "We think all beings should take responsibility for their own actions."

"You sound like my mother," I said, walking to the closet. It looked extremely weird, but that was mostly because everything was hung up very neatly—a sight I have never personally experienced.

The clothing was not all robes, as I had expected.

I Shrank My Teacher

Pleskit had a lot of things that were sort of like shirts and pants, though mostly they were stuck together to make one-piece outfits. The upper shelf held a collection of truly weird hats.

"Wild colors," I said.

"Thank you," said Pleskit, even though I hadn't meant it to be a compliment. "You know, the only reason I wore my ceremonial robe to school those first few days was because that traitor Mikta-makta-mookta told me it was the Fatherly One's desire. I did not realize she was just trying to make it harder for me to fit in." He pointed to a piece of clothing. "I thought I would wear this on Monday. It is more like the kind of garments your people wear. Therefore, I hope it will let me merge with the throng more successfully."

The thing he was pointing to did have pant legs, so it didn't look quite so much like a dress. On the other hand, it was a one-piece purple-and-green outfit covered with glittery spirals.

I hesitated for a moment, then said, "Uh . . . that's not going to do it, Pleskit. If we're going to get you to fit in better at school, the first thing we have to do is get you out of those clothes altogether."

He looked alarmed. "I cannot go to school naked!"

I felt myself blush. "No, no! I just mean we have to get you dressed in something that doesn't look so much like it came from another planet."

Personally, I thought Pleskit's clothes were pretty interesting. The robe he had worn on the first day of school had designs that moved on their own, illustrating stories from his homeworld. It was like wearing a video! Unfortunately, it also looked a little like a dress, which was more than some of the pinheads in our school could cope with.

"What do you suggest I should wear instead?" he asked.

"I dunno. Normal clothes, I guess. Maybe we should ask Linnsy about it."

Linnsy is my upstairs neighbor. She's in the same class as me, but is much higher on the social food chain. While I knew that Pleskit needed to change his look, asking *me* how to do it so that he would fit in better was like asking a goldfish how to build a bonfire.

"Let's go see her!" said Pleskit.

***

I Shrank My Teacher

Going anyplace with Pleskit is not entirely simple. This is because he has to be escorted by his bodyguard.

I asked Pleskit once what it was like having a bodyguard.

"I hate it!" he replied instantly. "I can't do anything without McNally tagging along. It is as if I had committed a Social Violation and been assigned a Keeper."

"A Keeper?" I asked, feeling confused.

Pleskit paused. "Ah, I forgot that you are still in the barbaric stage of Social Correction, and mostly use prisons." He paused and shuddered. "A Keeper is someone assigned to a person who has violated law or custom. It's how we guide a being to betterment after he, she, or it has fallen into social error. Which is one of the things that makes having a bodyguard so upsetting: It is as if I am the one who has committed the error! But that is not even the worst part."

"What is?" I asked, already startled by his answer.

"The fact that I have to have one at all. Think about it, Tim. It means that the people in charge here think there are other people who want to hurt, kidnap, or kill me! I do not like walking around with this idea always in my head. Also, I do not like what it says about this planet."

I didn't, either. But I also didn't want to get Pleskit started on what's wrong with Earth. Once he gets wound up, it's hard to get him to stop. So I just said, "Let's go get McNally."

Before long Pleskit, McNally, and I were on the way to my apartment building. We were taking the limo, which meant I would have to come back later to pick up my bike. That was okay with me. I was glad to have any excuse to go back to the embassy.

The limousine tunnel brought us out well past the circle of gawkers looking up at the embassy. Also, security sent out a couple of decoy limousines to draw off the reporters and stuff. So we made it to my place without much problem.

It was the first time I had brought Pleskit home, and I suddenly realized I should have called and let my mother know we were coming. But I had been so excited that it didn't occur to me. For a minute I thought maybe we should go directly to Linnsy's place. There was only one problem with that idea: *Her* mother was even more likely to wig out than mine was.

So we went to my apartment.

I Shrank My Teacher

My mother wigged anyway. Actually, she was pretty controlled about it. She only wigged a little when we came through the door. But after she had greeted Pleskit and McNally, she said, "Timothy, can I see you in the kitchen for a moment?"

Her neck was so tight the words barely made it through her lips.

I followed her into the kitchen.

"How could you do this to me?" she asked in an urgent whisper.

"You always tell me I should bring home more friends," I replied, trying to sound innocent.

"This isn't just a friend," she hissed. "It's an *alien!*"

I was disappointed. "I didn't expect you to be so prejudiced, Mom."

Her eyes got wide, and then she looked angry. "I am *not* upset because you brought an alien home! I'm upset because you didn't warn me so I could clean the house!"

Mothers. What can you do?

"Sorry," I said. "Next time I'll call first."

"Assuming you live that long," she said. "Come on—let's go be polite."

I followed her into the living room.

Pleskit and McNally were sitting on the couch. Pleskit was examining a clown my mother had made in her ceramics class. He looked up at her. "This is very terrifying," he said politely.

I wasn't sure, but I thought it was a compliment. Even so, my mother looked baffled, and a little hurt.

"We decided we needed to get Pleskit some normal clothes," I said. "So we came to talk to Linnsy about it."

My mother nodded. "She'll be a much better guide than you would."

I would have been insulted, except that this was incredibly true.

We called Linnsy, and she came down to our apartment.

"Well, there's only one thing to do!" she said gleefully. "It's time to take a trip to the mall!"

My mother turned to McNally. "Will that be safe?"

"I'll have to call for reinforcements," he replied.

Suddenly I realized that taking an alien to the shopping mall was going to be a lot more complicated than I had expected.

CHAPTER 7

[PLESKIT]
AT THE TEMPLE OF COMMERCE

It's a good thing that the limousine, which the Earthlings seem to love but which I find smelly and bumpy, is so big. By the time we left for the mall we had me, Tim, McNally, Tim's mother, and Linnsy all packed into the back. Fortunately, there was still lots of room.

Ralph the Driver raised his eyebrows when he saw us coming out of the building. But he didn't say anything. He never does.

Linnsy, who is taller than either Tim or me, seemed very excited by the trip. "You're gonna love this place, Pleskit," she kept telling me.

Indeed, I was truly amazed when we drove up to the mall. It was an enormous building, many, many times bigger than our school. The walls were covered with shiny glass, and it had a tall central section with a soaring spire.

"It is a temple of commerce!" I exclaimed. "A sacred place of business. Oh, Tim. For the first time I understand how truly your people value money and trade. Perhaps there is hope for our societies to connect after all."

"Money is not the only thing we value," said Mrs. Tompkins quickly. She sounded a little upset.

"It is not the only thing we value, either. But my father has taught me that all societies demonstrate what they value by what they build, and this is the biggest, most beautiful building I have seen since my arrival here. When I saw the school building, I feared your culture was not very advanced. But now that I see this tremendous structure, I understand your values better."

Mrs. Tompkins looked a little sad. She didn't say anything else, but I could tell I had upset her. Only I couldn't figure out how.

McNally was talking into a device in his hand as we

pulled up in front of the main entrance. "All right, see you guys inside" was the last thing I heard him say. Then he clicked the device shut, slipped it in his pocket, and opened the limousine door.

As we walked through the entrance, I saw two more men dressed just like McNally (and wearing the same kind of dark glasses) standing off on either side. Ahead of us was a moving stairway. At the top stood three more men, obviously also part of McNally's group.

I found it all a little scary.

The mall itself, though, was very pleasant. It had many stores selling strange and interesting items. The number of clothing stores astonished me, but also demonstrated to me that Tim was correct when he said that how I dressed was going to be important to getting along. External appearance seems to be an obsession among the Earthlings.

We passed an entire store devoted to soap. The smells were so strong that I nearly fainted. And the variety of messages I could read from those smells was astonishing—not to mention embarrassing. Yet my friends barely noticed them.

I was surprised by the number of kids I saw who

were doing nothing. And I was *terrified* when we passed a place where you could pay to have holes put in your ears!

I was also surprised by the things I did not see. When I asked for a poetry shop, Tim showed me a bookstore. When I asked about buying music, Linnsy pointed out a store filled with little packages filled with songs.

But where would you go to buy a fresh poem? I wondered. *Or to have someone sing your friend a brand-new song?*

There did not seem to be any *living* artists at the mall. Everything was packaged and brought in from somewhere else.

Tim insisted we go into a place called an arcade that truly confused me. It was filled with young people, and it was such a confusion of loud noises and flashing lights that I assumed it must be a room where children were sent to be punished. I was disturbed by the idea that Earthling parents could be so vicious.

I was surprised to realize that I was the only one who was screaming. In fact, even though most of the people were slapping the machines—which made sense to me—some of them actually seemed to be having a good time. (Others, however, had glazed looks on their faces, as if they had been placed under some mind-controlling drug.)

Then I saw that one of the machines was labeled "Alien Destruction" and had pictures of gruesome monsters on it.

"Look!" I cried in horror. "What does that mean?"

Tim and Linnsy quickly dragged me out of this torture chamber.

"Geez, Pleskit," said Tim, when we were outside. "It's just a game room."

I found this terrifying. If Earthlings play games like this in public, what kind of things do they do in private? I decided I did not want to think about it.

Things improved when we went to a place called a food court. Here I was almost overwhelmed by an astonishing variety of odors. I sampled several Earthling foods, including french fries (delicious!), ice cream (even better!), and something called ketchup, which comes in funny little packets that make it hard to get at, but was really the best thing of all. The strange part was, they gave *this* item away for free!

I was not able to get used to the fact that everywhere

we went people stared and pointed and whispered. But they didn't get too close, because McNally and his men wouldn't let them. Sometimes people would shout out, "We love you, Pleskit!"—which I thought was odd, since they had never actually met me. A few others shouted, "Go back where you came from, you alien freak!" which I thought was equally odd, for the same reason.

We were still eating when I heard someone say, "Come on, you guys, you can let me through. I go to school with him."

McNally looked over, then nodded to one of his agents. The man shrugged and lowered his arm, which he had been using to hold back a girl that I recognized from class. Her name is Misty Longacres. She has black hair that hangs nearly to her waist. Her eyes are large and dark. Her skin is a very pretty shade of brown, somewhat lighter than McNally's, but much darker than Tim's.

"Hi, Misty!" said Linnsy. Her voice sounded a little strained, and I could not tell if she was really happy to see Misty or not.

"Hi, guys," replied Misty. "What are you doing here?"

"Shopping for Pleskit," said Tim. "We're trying to help him fit in better."

I Shrank My Teacher

Misty looked at Tim in astonishment. *"You're* going to be his fashion consultant?"

Tim wrinkled his nose, which was some sort of Earthling signal I did not quite understand yet. "No, I'm just here to watch. Linnsy and my mother are going to do all the thinking on this one."

"Well, that's a relief," said Misty. She pulled up a chair and sat down next to us. "Listen, I got some news today." She looked around, then added dramatically, "You're *not* going to like it."

We waited in silence.

"Well, come on!" said Tim at last. "What is it?"

Some people clearly enjoy delivering bad news. Her eyes sparkling, Misty said, "Jordan's coming back. He'll be in school on Wednesday."

Tim's cry of horror caused several of McNally's men to pivot in our direction.

"Tim," said his mother sharply. "Control yourself." She had to look down to say this, because he had slid out of his seat and was lying flat on the floor.

"What's the point of controlling myself?" he moaned. "My life is over."

This statement made perfect sense to me. Given a

choice between Jordan returning to class and catching a horrible infectious disease, I would probably opt for the disease.

"I'm sure it's not going to be that bad," said Mrs. Tompkins. "Jordan probably learned a lesson after what happened last week."

"I doubt it, ma'am," said McNally. "My impression of that kid is that he's a born weasel, and he's going to stay a weasel no matter what happens to him."

Tim's mother shot McNally a look that was clearly meant to tell him to mind his own business.

"Where did you hear this?" demanded Linnsy.

Misty smiled. "My big sister told me. She's going out with Jordan."

"Jordan is too young to be going out!" said Mrs. Tompkins indignantly. "Especially with someone who's two years older than he is."

Misty just shrugged and cracked her gum.

I could contain myself no longer. "I am confused! Jordan is obviously a manifestation of the dark side of the universe. Why are they letting him back in school?"

"Oh, you gotta be a lot worse than Jordan to get kicked out of sixth grade," said Misty. "When my sister was in sixth, she had two kids in her class who had their own parole officers."

I tore open a ketchup package and sucked out the contents, which seemed to calm me a little.

Deciding there was no point in lingering at the table—my *clinkus* was so upset by the idea of Jordan coming back to class that I couldn't even finish my dessert—we went back to our shopping expedition.

Between all the new experiences and Misty's terrible news, I was already on edge. Then I saw the most horrifying thing of all. Grabbing Tim's arm, I screamed. "It's her! Look! It's her, *it's her!*"

CHAPTER 8

[TIM]
MISTAKEN IDENTITY

When Pleskit started to scream, McNally's men rushed to form a circle around us.

"Who?" I cried, glancing around in terror. "Who is it?"

"Mikta-makta-mookta!" cried Pleskit.

He was pointing at the window of a pet store. I stared at it for a minute, not understanding, then burst out laughing. "That's just a hamster!"

"A what?" asked Pleskit, obviously still frightened.

"A hamster. It's a pet—like your Veeblax."

Pleskit looked at me disbelievingly.

"I'll admit that it looks like Mikta-makta-mookta. But it's only two or three inches long.

Mikta-makta-mookta was taller than we are, Pleskit."

"What does height have to do with it? It's not like shrinking something is any big deal."

My mother put a hand on his shoulder. "This really is a very common pet on our planet, dear."

Pleskit moved closer to the window. "It would be a good place for Mikta-makta-mookta to hide," he said, still suspicious.

"Yeah, but look—the hamster's naked. Mikta-makta-mookta wouldn't go out in public like that, would she?"

"It depends on how desperate she was," said Pleskit. He pressed his face to the window, then sighed. "But I fear you are right, Tim. I have made a fool of myself. Again. That is not Mikta-makta-mookta. The eyes are different."

"Geez, kid," said McNally. "You scared me out of a year's growth."

"I thought you were already fully grown," said Pleskit, which caused Misty to giggle.

McNally sighed. "Let's go get your clothes."

Shopping with Pleskit turned out to be kind of fun, mostly because the clerks were incredibly attentive.

I Shrank My Teacher

Everyone—well, almost everyone—wanted to meet the alien and help him find the right things to wear. I had a feeling some of them were hoping they might be able to get him to do an advertisement: "Pleskit Meenom Shops Here," that kind of thing.

We got him four pairs of jeans, some T-shirts (including one that said JUST VISITING THIS PLANET, which Pleskit briefly thought had been made specifically for him), a sweatshirt, and a baseball cap.

The cap was a problem, of course, because of Pleskit's *sphen-gnut-ksher*, the knob that grows out of the top of his head. But McNally said he would cut a hole to make room for it, and my mother said if he did, she would stitch up the edges so it wouldn't tear.

We were all pretty tired by the time we left, but satisfied that we had done a good job. We gave Misty a ride to her home, then dropped off Mom and Linnsy at our apartment complex. I went back to the embassy with Pleskit and McNally so I could pick up my bike.

Ms. Buttsman was waiting for us in the kitchen. Her eyes had all the warmth of a package of ice cubes. "I can't believe you did that, Mr. McNally."

McNally looked puzzled. "Did what?"

"Took Pleskit to the mall. The mall of all places! There is no need for the boy to be exposed to the public like that. The better clothing stores would have been glad to bring their items here."

"Chill," said McNally, which seemed to really infuriate Ms. Buttsman. "The kid got a little taste of Earthling culture."

"A very nice taste," put in Pleskit. "Ketchup is a superior foodstuff. We should stock up on it."

Ignoring him, Ms. Buttsman glared at McNally. "I intend to have a serious conversation with Meenom Ventrah about this!"

McNally stifled a yawn. "Yeah, whatever you want. If you'll excuse me, I'm off duty now."

And with that he turned and walked away.

Ms. Buttsman sighed in exasperation. "That man and I are not going to get along," she muttered.

Actually, I was beginning to doubt that Ms. Buttsman got along with anyone. But I kept the thought to myself. I already suspected that she didn't like me. I didn't want to give her anything additional to hold against me. I was afraid she might bar me from the embassy.

Pleskit led me back to the little transport room. I

took the silver tube to the blue-domed guard shack, where I picked up my bicycle.

It was getting dark now. As I was riding away from the park, I noticed a smallish man standing under a tree. He waved to me, and I realized that I had seen him at the mall, more than once—almost as if he had been following us.

"Hey, Tim," he called. "I want to talk to you for a minute."

I hesitated. His voice was friendly. But I had no idea who he was—or why he would know my name.

"Sorry!" I called. "I gotta get home."

I started riding faster. At the edge of the park I glanced back over my shoulder.

The man was about twenty feet behind me—which surprised me, since he was on foot, and I was riding.

I began pumping the pedals as hard as I could. Behind me I heard a shout of anger. I glanced over my shoulder again. The man was running—running faster than I would have thought possible.

Cold fear blossomed in my gut, and I began pedaling even harder. My bike bounced and jolted as I blasted over potholes, jumped curbs, spun around corners.

I heard the man shouting, but his voice was beginning to fade. I didn't slow down—and I didn't head straight for home. Just because this guy knew my name, didn't mean he knew where I lived, and I saw no reason to lead him there. I shot down Ackerman, turned on Lancaster, then zigged over to Westcott Street.

When I was sure I had lost him, I headed for home. My calf muscles were burning and my lungs felt as if they had been sandpapered. But I felt really good about managing to elude the guy.

When I got home, I called Pleskit and told him what had happened. We talked about it for a long time. Finally we decided the guy was probably just a reporter.

Even so, I didn't sleep very well that night.

CHAPTER 9

[PLESKIT]
THE WORM (RE)TURNS

The Earthlings divide their time into seven-
day cycles called weeks.

Our shopping trip was on the day they call Saturday.

On the next day, which is called Sunday, I stayed home doing schoolwork and playing "Interstellar Trader" on the embassy's computer. The Earthlings had given us some devices called cell phones, and I used mine to talk to Tim a couple of times. These phones are useful, but very primitive. I decided to ask the Fatherly One if we could give Tim and his mother something more sophisticated, so that I could at least smell Tim when I am talking to him.

On the next day; which is called Monday, it was time to go to school again. I was excited, because I hoped this would be a better week than my first week—especially since I felt that Tim, Linnsy, and Misty were all my friends now.

I put on some of my new clothes. The jeans felt rough and stiff against my skin, but I was willing to put up with that if it would help me fit in.

Unfortunately, I had some trouble getting past Ms. Buttsman with my new clothes.

"Pleskit!" she cried when she saw me. "You're not going to school like that, are you? You really ought to dress more properly; at least go back and put on a white shirt and a tie!"

"But none of the other kids dress formally."

"That is no reason to demean yourself or the planet you represent. You should set an example for the others."

"I don't want to set an example! I just want to fit in! I thought that was one of your jobs—to help me fit in with the Earthlings. Or are you going to sabotage me like Mikta-makta-mookta did?"

Ms. Buttsman looked pained. "My job is to advise

you and your father on proper protocol. Your father has already shown a disregard for that in his insistence that you attend a public school when there are so many fine private schools available. Obviously, I can only do so much. But I must at least make my opinions known."

McNally, who had been listening to this conversation, said, "In my opinion, you should give the kid a break."

Ms. Buttsman's nostrils grew wide, which I took to indicate indignation. "*You* are not being paid for your opinion, Mr. McNally."

"That's true. But I am being paid to get Pleskit to school on time—and to make sure that he doesn't get the crap kicked out of him once he's there. The first part calls for me to get him out of here now. The second part will be easier if he's not dressed like a dork. Come on, Pleskit. Let's go."

I smiled at Ms. Buttsman as I walked past.

She smiled back, but I could tell she didn't mean it.

"That woman is going to drive me out of my mind," muttered McNally when we were in the limousine.

"Tim calls her 'The Butt,'" I said.

McNally laughed. "That's nicer than *my* name for her."

I asked what his name for her was, but he wouldn't tell me.

When I walked through the door, my teacher, Ms. Weintraub, said, "Why, Pleskit—you've assimilated!"

A cold fear seized my heart and I felt my *clinkus* begin to shrivel. Clutching her hands, I cried, "You don't really mean it, do you? Please, say you don't mean it!"

She looked baffled. "I only meant that you are dressing like the other kids. I think it looks quite nice."

I relaxed, but just a little. "Perhaps I did not understand. When we speak of 'assimilating' we mean someone has abandoned his home planet and given himself over to another culture. It is one of the greatest crimes a diplomat—or one of his family—can commit. If my father thought I was assimilating he would *splork*."

Ms. Weintraub laughed. "I'm sorry, Pleskit. We use the phrase more casually here. I did not mean to offend you."

"I was more terrified than offended," I replied. "But now I understand. Thank you, Ms. Weintraub."

I heard a few giggles behind me while this was going on, but when I turned, most of the kids just looked sort of wide-eyed and confused. I saw Tim, Linnsy, and Misty, which made me feel somewhat safer—especially when Tim nodded in greeting, Linnsy gave me a little wave, and Misty smiled and tilted her head. I was not alone. This *was* going to be a better week!

Hah! If I had only known. . . .

Even so, things did start well.

On Monday at recess Tim, Misty, and Linnsy all spent time with me. And Misty introduced me to another boy named Chris Mellblom who was pretty funny and knew some interesting tricks to do with coins. I enjoyed seeing them. As the Fatherly One always says, "Tricky is good."

On Tuesday we had a class called physical education. I did not participate because no one had told me that I was going to have to bring a pair of short pants.

"Looks like we'll have to make another trip to the mall," said Linnsy afterward.

"Don't mind her," said Tim. "She always thinks it's time to go to the mall."

Watching physical education, I learned that Earthlings have a special sport called gymnastics, which involves a lot of bending and bouncing of the body. Linnsy told me that our school has a team for it. "I'm on it," she said proudly. "So are Misty and Rafaella. And Ms. Weintraub is our coach."

"Ms. Weintraub?" I asked in surprise.

"She was a national competitor when she was in high school," said Misty. "Almost made it to the Olympics!"

Alas, after two good days Wednesday arrived, and with it the event Tim and I had been dreading.

Jordan Lynch returned to school.

Despite my hopes, my new look was not enough to shield me from his poisonous tongue. The first afternoon he approached me on the playground. Brad Kent, the kid Tim always calls Jordan's "second-in-command," was tagging along behind him.

They stopped in front of me. Jordan looked me up and down for a minute, then said, "Nice outfit, Plesk-o."

"Thank you, Jordan," I replied, feeling slightly surprised.

"I was wondering," he continued. "Do you really think jeans and a T-shirt can turn you into an Earthling?"

The tone of Jordan's voice was almost friendly.

Even so, his words cut like a knife. Not because I want to be an Earthling, but because they were meant to use my differentness against me.

"You think *anything* could turn you into a human being?" replied Tim.

Jordan rolled his eyes. "Worms should not speak unless spoken to." He turned and walked away. "Second-in-command" trotted after him, patting him on the back and telling him how brilliant he was.

I was so unhappy about having to deal with Jordan that I actually went to Ms. Buttsman for advice, figuring that manners and protocol are her specialty.

Though she seemed happy to be consulted, her advice ("Smile politely, tell him that what he said was inappropriate, and ask him not to repeat the offense") was not really effective.

To be more precise, when I tried it, it caused Jordan to burst into uncontrollable laughter.

Then, to make things even worse, on Thursday afternoon I got . . . The Note.

CHAPTER 10

[TIM]
ALIEN BIOLOGY

As we were leaving the classroom for recess on Thursday, Pleskit sidled over to me and said, "Tim! I must speak to you on a matter of great urgency."

"Cool," I said, wondering if some interplanetary crisis had come up.

It was a crisis all right, but not interplanetary. Leading me to a secluded spot, he pulled a folded piece of paper from his jeans and said, "Read this."

I looked at the note. It was written on lavender paper. It said, "Dear Pleskit: I think purple is a hot color. I also think you are a very cute boy."

It was signed, "Love, Misty." She had used a little heart to dot the *i* in her name.

Dear Pleskit,
I think purple is a ~~hot~~ color. I also think ~~you~~ are a <u>very</u> <u>cute</u> boy.
Love, Misty

"Uh-oh," I said. "You're in trouble, buddy."

He groaned. "That is what I feared. What should I do?"

"Geez, don't ask me. I never got a note like that. I know! Let's talk to Linnsy. She understands this kind of thing."

I went looking for Linnsy, and dragged her back to where Pleskil was waiting.

Fingers trembling, he handed her the letter. "Look!" he said, sounding pitiful.

Linnsy glanced at it, then shrugged. "You aren't surprised, are you?"

"Of course I am surprised! I am . . ." Pleskit paused and rolled his eyes up, as if he was looking for a word somewhere inside his brain. "I am *flabbergasted!*"

Linnsy laughed and shook her head. "I can't believe how clueless you two are! Honestly, if it was up to guys, the species would probably die out completely."

"I am not part of this species," said Pleskit reasonably.

"Well, how do they do things on your planet?" asked Linnsy.

"Before or after the egg?"

"You guys come out of eggs?" I yelped. "That is so neat!"

"Well, not entirely," said Pleskit. "The shells create quite a mess."

I sighed. "I don't mean neat as in tidy. I mean neat as in . . . cool!"

"Don't start in on *cool* again!" cried Pleskit. "I already have enough to think about!"

"Ignore Tim," said Linnsy. "He's just here for background noise. I still want to know about dating and stuff on your planet."

"Well, it's mostly handled by the *feebrix*," said Pleskit.

"The what?" I asked.

"The *feebrix* is the being that connects a Fatherly One with a Motherly One."

"Sort of like a dating service?" asked Linnsy.

Pleskit paused to consider this. "No, the *feebrix* is more like a six-legged treesnake that—"

"Stop right there!" cried Linnsy. "I don't think I want to know about this after all. Let's just try to deal with this letter." She looked at it again, and furrowed her brow suspiciously. "Hmmm. There's something weird about this. Pleskit, how do you feel about Misty?"

"I like her."

"Wait, Pleskit," I said warningly. "I don't think you entirely understand the question. Linnsy means do you like Misty . . . well, you know. The way she likes you."

Pleskit blinked, and a smell something like rotten eggs mixed with strawberry jam came out of his *sphen-gnut-ksher*. It was so strong that Linnsy and I started to cough.

"Sorry," he said. "That is the odor of extreme alarm.

No, I do not like Misty that way. I cannot! It is forbidden! The Fatherly One would *sprindle a glixxit* if he even thought I was considering such a thing."

"Well, I guess that clarifies things," I said.

"Not really," said Linnsy. "Look, I've got a bad feeling about this letter. It's a good thing you asked me for advice. I'll talk to Misty myself and report back to you later."

She turned to go—and bumped right into Jordan Lynch.

It really bugs me that someone as skeezy as Jordan is so tall and good looking. Why couldn't his face reflect his personality? (Well, I know the answer to that, actually. You can't put the face of a weasel on the body of a human being.)

"Where did you come from?" sputtered Linnsy.

Jordan shrugged. "I noticed the meeting of the nerd pack and wondered what was going on. You looked upset."

"As if that would bother you," I sneered.

Jordan put his hand on his heart. "Tim, you wound me. Of course I care. Why, think what it would mean if—for example—someone in class was in love with

Pleskit and he didn't know what to do about it." He began to snicker.

"Jordan!" cried Pleskit. "Have you been reading my mail?"

Jordan laughed. "And do you believe everything you read, Pleskit? Like a love letter from Misty? As if! Sorry if I disturbed you, Ples; this has actually been part of a scientific study. I was checking to see how gullible aliens really are. The answer seems to be—extremely!"

Still laughing, he started to walk away. Suddenly he turned back and said, "Hey, Linnsy—keep hanging around with losers like Tim and Purplebutt and people are going to start thinking you might be a nerd, too."

"Why don't you go back to your slime pit before you dry out and your skin starts to split," said Linnsy.

Jordan raised his eyebrows in mock surprise, then turned and wandered off, still chuckling to himself.

"He is in desperate need of an attitude readjustment," said Pleskit. Then, looking worried, he added, "Are there many people on your planet like him?"

"Enough," said Linnsy.

Pleskit frowned. "That is a very alarming thought!"

***

Jordan didn't let up, of course. Except that on Friday he directed his nastiness more at me than at Pleskit.

"Hey, Tompkins," he said as we were walking into the building that morning. "You think you're really a big deal because you hang around with that purple kid, don't you?"

I shrugged. "Not really."

Jordan snorted. "Yeah, not really. Well, don't let it go to your head. You could spend the day in a refrigerator and you still wouldn't be cool."

By the time the day was over, Jordan had managed to get three major laughs at my expense.

Pleskit was furious. "Do you know why he's picking on you so much?" he asked me that day at recess.

"Habit, probably. He's been doing it since he moved here two years ago."

"That may be part of it. But I think it's even worse than usual right now because Ms. Weintraub has told him not to talk to me. That is good for me, but bad for you. Therefore, I think we should do something about it."

"I've wanted to do something about it for two years. Got any great ideas?"

I Shrank My Teacher

Pleskit looked from side to side. "Can you come home with me this afternoon?"

"Should be okay, as long as I let Mom know where I'm going to be. She doesn't get home from work until about six anyway."

"We can call her from the limousine," said Pleskit. "If she says no, we will just drive you home instead. But I hope she says yes. I've decided that we should have a talk with the Grandfatherly One."

Pleskit's Grandfatherly One actually died quite a while ago, but they kept his brain so that they can consult him on difficult matters. At least, that was the plan. But the first time I met him, he was pretty cranky about the fact that Pleskit's Fatherly One pretty much ignores him. I got the impression he was actually happy to have us ask him questions, just because it gave him someone to talk to.

"What are we going to talk to him about?" I asked.

"I want the Grandfatherly One to advise us on dealing with Jordan."

"Your Grandfatherly One has lived all over the galaxy. He's a mighty brain. Why would he bother with something like this?"

"Because he's bored. Also, he hates bullies."

So we went to visit the brain of Pleskit's Grand-fatherly One.

And Pleskit was right.

He gave us a truly cool suggestion.

Who would have guessed it would end up getting us in so much trouble?

CHAPTER 11

[P L E S K I T]
BRAINSTORM

To visit the Grandfatherly One, we moved very quietly and took a couple of smaller hallways that go around the side of the embassy. The reason for this was simple: We did not want to run into Ms. Buttsman. Life was just easier if we could avoid her.

The Grandfatherly One lives in a large liquid-filled tank that has a viewing device and speakers on the side. Because the Fatherly One has ordered all of us in the embassy to speak the language of our host country as long as we are here, the tank's computer has been programmed so that the words of the Grandfatherly One come out in English.

"Been wondering what was up with you two," he said when we entered. "I've been pretty bored for the last couple of days."

I realized, with a good deal of guilt, that I had not filled him in on what had happened to us since the last time we visited him. So Tim and I quickly told the story of how Mikta-makta-mookta had nearly sucked our brains out, and how we had escaped and unmasked both her and the traitor Harr-giss.

"Well done!" he said when we were finished. "Now, I suppose the fact that you've come to see me again means you have another problem. You know, thoughtless youngling, it would be nice if you came to visit sometimes just to see me, or because you wanted to lessen the terrible burden of my loneliness."

The first part of his request was valid. The second part was right over the top. "Please, O Venerated One," I replied, "do not play guilt games with my mind."

This caused him to chuckle. "You're learning, sprout. But my point remains valid. Simple respect and kindness should drive you here to visit me more often."

"I will try to improve in that regard, Grandfatherly

One. However, in the meantime, you are correct—we do have another problem."

Quickly Tim and I outlined what it was like having Jordan back in class.

"I know the type," said the Grandfatherly One. "Believe it or not, with proper direction he could become a strong and positive adult being. Left uncorrected . . ."

The Grandfatherly One let the sentence hang in the air until Tim finally cried, "What? What?"

"He has the potential to become a force of evil—small evil if he does not advance in the world, great evil if he rises to power. It would be good to cut him down to size a bit—not only for your sake, but for his own sake, and the sake of the future of this world."

"I always knew Jordan was more dangerous than my mother would admit," said Tim, sounding satisfied.

"If you are agreed that he is a danger, then how do you suggest we deal with him?" I asked the Grandfatherly One.

"You must learn to pay more attention, Pleskit. I have already answered that question."

"What do you mean?"

"Think about it," said the Grandfatherly One. Then he pulled in his visual unit and shut down his speaker.

"Is he all right?" asked Tim in alarm.

"He is fine," I replied.

"Well, what happened?"

"He is pretending to be asleep. That means he is done talking to us and wants me to figure out what he meant on my own. It's an old trick of his." I turned back to the bottle. "Good-bye, Grandfatherly One. I shall go and contemplate your wisdom."

He did not answer.

We went to my room to jump on the bed while I thought about the riddle posed by the Grandfatherly One.

"Okay, let's see if we can remember exactly what he said," suggested Tim.

"No need to remember it," I said. "I can simply replay it."

"Is this place bugged?" asked Tim. He looked alarmed.

"We have no insects that I know of," I replied. "Why do you ask?"

"Well, how are you going to replay what your

I Shrank My Teacher

Grandfatherly One said to us if you didn't record it somehow?" Then he blinked and smiled. "Oh, I've got it! You use your *sphen-gnut-ksher*, right? I forgot about that."

"Yes, exactly. Come on—let's go see if we can figure this out."

I bounced off the bed and went to my desk. The Veeblax was sitting next to my download box, and it had inflated itself enough to do a nearly perfect imitation of the black cube. It took me a minute to figure out which was which; once I had it, I picked up the wrong one, as if by accident. The Veeblax chuckled and switched back to its basic form. I jumped and pretended it had fooled me, which made it chuckle even harder.

"That thing could be dangerous," said Tim nervously.

"All things are dangerous, if you know how to use them properly," I replied. I picked up the download box, adjusted the appropriate dial so that it would record only the events of the last hour, then inserted my *sphen-gnut-ksher.* Once I had it comfortably in place, I pushed the Start button.

The box hummed and grew warm as memories poured into the holding tank.

When the box beeped twice to indicate that it was done, I pulled out my *sphen-gnut-ksher* and put the box into the playback device. Then I put on my goggles to review the conversation with the Grandfatherly One. When I was done I handed the goggles to Tim and let him watch, too.

"*That* is *extremely* freaky," he said when he removed the goggles.

I was offended by these words, until I realized that since Tim is basically nice, this was more likely another strange use of language, and not him trying to insult me.

"I do not care if it is . . . freaky," I said. "I just care that we figure out what the Grandfatherly One was suggesting."

"I don't know," said Tim. "The only thing he actually said we should do to Jordan was cut him down to size."

"Of course!" I cried. "That's it! Why didn't I realize it to begin with?"

CHAPTER 12

[TIM]

DESK TOYS OF MASS DESTRUCTION

"What?" I cried. "What's *it?*"

"The Grandfatherly One said we should cut Jordan down to size."

"Yeah? So are we going to slice off his legs at the knees or something?"

Pleskit looked shocked. "That would be barbaric! No, we're simply going to shrink him."

I tried to keep my eyes from bugging out. "How are we going to do that?"

Pleskit's face turned serious. From his *sphen-gnut-ksher* came that faint smell of fish that I have come to realize means that he is thinking. "Hmmm. That is a matter for some consideration. The shrinking ray Is a fairly simple device. On the other hand, it is kept on the desk of the Fatherly One—it's one of his toys."

"A toy?" I asked in surprise.

"The job of the Fatherly One carries great responsibility. He needs ways to relieve the tensions."

Ignoring the fact that this "toy" was something most Earth scientists would gladly sacrifice a body part in order to examine, I said, "Do you suppose he'll let us use it?"

Pleskit shook his head glumly. "That is about as likely as my being invited back to Geembol Seven."

This sort of irritated me, because I know that something awful happened on that planet, but he won't tell me what.

"Well," I said, "that means we're right back where we started."

Pleskit smiled. "I said I did not think he would loan it to us. But one of the earliest things the Fatherly One taught me was that it is easier to get forgiveness than it is to get permission."

"That's a weird thing for a parent to tell you," I said.

"The Fatherly One wants me to become an effective

adult. He thinks Earthlings are very odd in this regard. Many of the traits that you admire in grown-ups, such as standing up for yourself, or speaking your own mind, are things that people really dislike in kids. He is very interested in trying to figure out how any of you survive your childhoods. Anyway, since the Grandfatherly One has suggested it, I think we should simply borrow the shrinking device."

"You've got to be kidding!" I squawked, wondering what the punishment was for borrowing an alien diplomat's desk toy without his permission.

"I could not be more serious. Remember, we may well be all that stands between Jordan and the path of great evil."

Which is how I ended up following my alien friend into the office of his Fatherly One. Of course, we couldn't have gotten in if Meenom had been there. But according to Pleskit he was often gone, making visits to presidents, premiers, and prime ministers.

"Your father meets all the most important people in the world," I said in awe.

"It's his job," said Pleskit, as if it was no big deal.

The other thing that made it easier to get into

Meenom's office was that he did not yet have a new secretary to replace the traitorous Mikta-makta-mookta.

I had seen the office before, when Pleskit and his Fatherly One gave me, my mother, and Linnsy a tour of the embassy. Even so, I found it awesome. The outer wall of the room is curved, much like the one in Pleskit's bedroom. But, being on the main floor of the embassy, this wall is much bigger. When the windows are clear, they give an amazing view of the city. Now they were set to show an image of another world. It was a city, still, but one with strangely rounded buildings topped by unimaginably high towers, streets that were nearly empty, and skies that were crowded with what Pleskit called "Personal Flying Vehicles."

About five feet above the center of the room floated Meenom Ventrah's command pod, where he sat when he was working at home. In the center of the pod was a deeply padded chair. This was surrounded by a clear blue shell. At the front of the shell was an opening about two feet wide. The chair's armrests held keypads where Meenom could enter commands and queries. The responses appeared on the wall in front of him.

"So where does your Fatherly One keep his desk toys?" I asked.

"Watch," said Pleskit. He held out his hands and cracked his knuckles in a tricky little rhythm. The command pod began to descend. When it reached floor level, Pleskit scrambled into the seat. He touched a knob on one of the control pads, and the pod returned to its original position. Then he touched another knob. A slot in the wall opened. Out slid a shelf made of the same clear blue material as the command pod. It floated across the room, coming to a stop right in front of the pod's opening. On the shelf lay about a dozen totally fascinating-looking gadgets. If not for the fact that I was terrified of being caught in here, I would have begged Pleskit to explain them all to me.

"Ah, here we go," he said, picking up the least interesting-looking item—a red box about the size of a large grapefruit. "Catch, Tim."

"Wait!" I cried in terror. "Don't!"

Too late. He had tossed the box down to me.

It slipped through my hands and hit the floor.

"What have you done?" cried Pleskit in alarm.

"I tried to tell you—I can't catch!"

Quickly he returned the pod to floor level. I had already picked up the box and was checking it for cracks or dents.

Pleskit took it from me. "You can't catch?" he asked in surprise. He sounded amused.

"Don't rub it in," I said, turning my head away. I get sick of being teased over the fact that I am a total klutz.

"This is a great relief to me," continued Pleskit. "I thought from the culture tapes I had experienced that all Earthlings were very physically adept. I am clumsy, too. I am so glad to know I am not the only one on the planet."

I smiled, just a little. "So, did I break the shrinking ray?" I asked nervously.

Pleskit shook the thing. "I do not think so. By the way, the proper technical term for this device is *Molecule Compactor.*"

"Why?"

"Well, because that's how it works. If you have studied the structure of an atom, you know that even the most solid-looking things are mostly made up of empty space."

"Uh, I guess so," I said, feeling a little guilty about the fact that I had read so much more science fiction than actual science.

Pleskit must have caught my uncertainty, because he expanded his explanation. "The atoms from which things are made are arranged something like a solar system. In the center is the nucleus, which is like the 'star' of the system. Orbiting it, pretty much the way planets orbit the sun, are electrons. Between them lies empty space. An atom is so tiny you might not think that space would amount to much, but if you enlarged an atom so that the nucleus was the size of, oh, an apple, then the closest of its electrons would be about *five miles away!* So you can see that most of what things are is . . . nothing! The Molecule Compactor simply squeezes out some of that empty space. Of course, that means that when you shrink something, it keeps its original weight, since nothing is lost but the emptiness. No matter how small you make a hundred-pound person, he will still weigh a hundred pounds."

"Cool!" I said. "So, how small *can* we make Jordan?"

I Shrank My Teacher

Pleskit closed his eyes for a second, as if he was consulting some in-brain data bank, then said, "We should probably not bring him down to less than two inches. The compactor *could* make him smaller. But the side effects would be . . . unpleasant."

"Two inches is fine!" I said gleefully. "Uh—I hate to ask this, but how do we bring him back?"

"Oh, we don't have to worry about *that*. The forces involved are so tremendous that the compacting can only last for a few hours. He will enlarge on his own—though it would be best if he is not in an enclosed spot when that happens. Now, come on—let's get out of here before someone comes in."

Tucking the Molecule Compactor under his arm, Pleskit led the way to the door.

As we stepped into the hall, I froze in terror.

CHAPTER 13

[PLESKIT]
THE PLAN IN ACTION

"Well, boys," said Ms. Buttsman, when she saw Tim and me coming out of the Fatherly One's office. "And just what are *you* doing here?"

I wanted to ask her the same question. Instead, I said, "I left one of my . . . my . . ."

"Toys!" prompted Tim.

"Yes, one of my *toys* in the office of the Fatherly One. I wanted to show it to Tim. So we came to retrieve it."

Ms. Buttsman narrowed her eyes. "That doesn't look much like a toy to me, Pleskit."

Tim laughed nervously. "Of course it doesn't! It's from another planet. It's bound to be different."

I Shrank My Teacher

Ms. Buttsman's face grew stern and cold—or, to be more precise, even sterner and colder than usual. Pointing a finger at Tim, she said, "Young man, you have been given a great privilege in being allowed to visit this embassy. It is imperative that you adhere to certain standards. Official government policy is that we are at all times to emphasize the similarities between our peoples, and not the differences. Please keep that in mind. If you cannot, I will have to take steps to prevent you from coming here."

This made me so mad it was all I could do to keep myself from turning the shrinking ray on Ms. Buttsman right then and there. Tim was doing his interesting trick of turning bright red.

A tweeting sound came from Ms. Buttsman's pocket. She took out a small device, flipped it open, held it to her ear, and snapped, "Buttsman here." She listened for a second, then covered the part she held to her mouth. "It's the president. You boys run along. And please remember what I said, Timothy."

As we turned to go, I farted the small and nasty fart of disrespect. I knew she would not be able to interpret it properly, but it made me feel better anyway.

***

Back in my room we tested the Molecule Compactor on the Veeblax. It quickly reduced the creature to about the size of my little finger.

"That rocks!" cried Tim.

"I would have shrunk it as much as we are going to shrink Jordan," I said. "But I was afraid we would not be able to find it."

"Gleep!" shrieked the Veeblax in a very tiny voice. "Gleep! Gleep! Gleep!"

Feeling somewhat guilty for alarming the creature, I let it crawl into my hand, where it seemed to feel safe.

"Okay," said Tim. "Next question: How do we get Jordan in position to use this on him?"

I emitted the smell of puzzlement. "I had not thought about that. We cannot do it in front of the rest of the class."

"Time to call in reinforcements," said Tim.

It took me a moment to realize that he meant it was time to ask Linnsy for advice.

"You guys are crazy," said Linnsy after we explained our plan.

"Does that mean you won't help?" asked Tim. She

smiled. "No, it just means I think you're crazy. But I want to see Jordan get cut down to size as much as you do. Enough that I'm even willing to get involved in one of Tim's nutty schemes—which is saying a lot, since normally I would rather have red-hot needles stuck under my fingernails than get involved in one of his wacko plans."

"That is a very strong statement!" I cried.

"Wait until you've been here awhile, Pleskit," she said. "Tim has a gift for getting in trouble in truly weird ways."

I looked at Tim with new respect. Maybe we had even more in common than I realized.

We were sitting in Tim's apartment. McNally was in the kitchen, having coffee with Tim's mother. This not only made him happy—Shhh-foop still had not learned to make coffee my bodyguard could drink—it also left us free to make our plans, as long as we kept our voices low. Tim and I had considered inviting Linnsy to the embassy to talk, but did not think there was anyplace we could sit where we would be free of the prying ears of Ms. Buttsman.

Linnsy was pacing back and forth in front of the

television set. "Okay, to begin with you need to do this when no one else is around to see it happen—which probably means you guys need to stay in the classroom when we go out for recess."

"How are we going to do that?" asked Tim.

Linnsy rolled her eyes. "How about trying your usual method, doofus? Don't get your work done."

Tim scowled, but admitted that that probably would work.

"The bigger trick will be getting McNally out of the way," continued Linnsy. "He sticks to you like glue, Pleskit."

"Of course he does. It's his job."

We sat, staring at one another, trying to figure out a way to get McNally to leave us alone long enough to shrink Jordan. But none of us could come up with an answer. Finally Tim looked up and said, "Okay, we've got to break the box."

I was alarmed. "What is the point of breaking the box, after all the trouble we went through to get it?"

He shook his head. "I'm not talking about the Molecule Compactor. I'm talking about the thinking box."

"Well, *that* explains everything," said Linnsy.

I Shrank My Teacher

"I'm serious," said Tim. "It's a tactic my uncle taught me for solving brainteasers and stuff. If you get stuck trying to find the answer, try looking at the question in a completely different way. For example, we're stuck on trying to figure out how to get rid of McNally. So let's change the question: Is there some way we could do this *without* getting rid of him?"

"Maybe we could ask him to help," I said.

Tim started to laugh.

"I'm not joking," I said, feeling a trifle cranky.

Tim blinked. He glanced toward the kitchen. "You know, it just might work!"

"Are you *serious!*" asked Linnsy.

"McNally is cool," said Tim. "He might actually go for it."

"Well, you guys know him better than I do. If you can get McNally to go along with it, and if you can get yourselves stuck inside during recess, then I'll do what I can to get Jordan back into the classroom."

She held out her hand. Tim placed his on top of it.

Clearly, this was some sort of ritual.

I reached out and put my hand on top of theirs.

The pact was made.

***

When I brought up the subject to McNally on the way back to the embassy, he began to laugh. "Let me get this straight, Pleskit. You want me to look the other way so you can *shrink* Jordan?"

I nodded. "That is the basic plan."

He shook his head. "That's the craziest thing I ever heard." He turned and looked out the window for a minute. When he turned back, his face was very serious. "I had a kid like Jordan in my class when I went to school. More than one of them. They made my life miserable, until I got big enough and strong enough to get them off my back."

He looked away again and didn't say anything else for a while. But when we got back to the embassy, he said, "You sure this shrinky-thing won't hurt Jordan?"

"The device is guaranteed safe for all living creatures."

McNally nodded. "Well, if you and Tim do happen to find yourselves stuck inside during recess tomorrow . . . let's just say some openings might arise. But you'd better have a good excuse if anything happens. Because you and I never had this conversation. Understand?"

"I understand," I said solemnly.

I Shrank My Teacher

I could hardly sleep that night, I was so filled with excitement.

The next day I carefully put the Molecule Compactor in my backpack.

When Tim got to class, he looked at me and raised his eyebrows. I had learned enough about human communication to know this was a question. I answered it by nodding. Tim smiled.

We did not finish our work, and Ms. Weintraub told us to stay in.

Linnsy glanced back at us as she left the room. I nodded to her, to let her know I had the device.

As soon as everyone was gone, Tim and I set the Molecule Compactor on one of the front desks and aimed its beam at the door.

McNally was at the back of the room, staring out the window.

We heard someone coming.

I stood at the machine, tense and eager.

Tim stood at the door, ready to push it closed, so Jordan could not escape.

The knob turned.

The door opened.

"Now!" cried Tim.

I flicked the switch, and the compacting beam shot out.

"Wait!" screamed Tim. "Pleskit, *wait!*"

It was too late.

I gasped as I realized what a horrible mistake we had just made.

CHAPTER 14

[T I M]
CATASTROPHE!

I was so excited about the chance to shrink Jordan that I wasn't paying as much attention as I should have. So I was a couple of seconds late in realizing that it wasn't Jordan who had walked through the door.

It was Ms. Weintraub.

I shouted for Pleskit to turn off the shrinking beam. At the same moment I rushed forward, trying to shove her out of the beam's path. I hit her at exactly the same instant the beam did; hit her, but not hard enough. She stayed in the beam—and so did I.

Which meant that we *both* shrank.

It was one of the oddest things I have ever experienced. It didn't hurt, actually. But I felt a kind of heaviness, an enormous pressure, as if I was being squeezed by a giant hand. At the same time I felt as if something was being pulled out of me, so that I was collapsing in on myself, the way a soda bottle does when you suck the air out of it.

The floor seemed to be rushing at me. The walls shot up around me until the ceiling seemed as distant as the sky.

And then it was over.

Ms. Weintraub was, shall we say, not amused. "Tim!" she screamed. "What's happening?"

Her tiny voice was high and squeaky. Any other time it would have sounded funny, but right now I was in no mood to laugh. I looked up at the huge and strange new world around us. "Well," I said in a voice that would have embarrassed Mickey Mouse, "we, uh, we, uh, we, uh, we sort of shrunk."

"Sort of?" Ms. Weintraub screeched. *"Sort of?!?* We're two inches tall!"

Things look vastly different when you are that height. Ms. Weintraub's desk, which was off to my right, looked like a giant office building. The pencil on the floor next to me was like a yellow log. And the blackboard eraser lying nearby would have made a good mattress, if it hadn't been so dusty.

Suddenly McNally and Pleskit were lying on the floor, staring at us in horror. Their faces loomed over us like monuments. Ms. Weintraub walked to McNally. Even though he had his chin on the floor, her head came only to the edge of his lip.

"What do you have to do with this?" she demanded.

"I'm just an innocent bystander," he said, sounding incredibly guilty.

"Hah!" She turned to Pleskit. Putting her hands on her hips, she said, "Just what is this all about, anyway?"

"We were going to shrink Jordan," said Pleskit miserably. "We thought it would teach him a lesson."

Ms. Weintraub groaned, buried her face in her hands, and muttered, "They told me having you in my class would be an adventure."

"I'm sorry," said Pleskit.

"Me, too!" I squeaked.

"Skip the apologies! Just make me big again."

Pleskit looked more miserable than ever. "We can't."

"What?"

"The machine doesn't have a reverse switch. You just have to wait for it to wear off."

"How long is *that* going to take?"

"Two or three hours."

I Shrank My Teacher

Ms. Weintraub slumped to the floor—not that far, given her current height. I really like her, and when I saw her sitting there, shoulders bent, face hidden, I felt about as lousy as I have ever felt. I was still trying to get up the nerve to apologize again when she straightened her back and said, "All right, we have to figure out how we're going to get through the next few hours until Tim and I return to normal."

"Get through them?" asked McNally and Pleskit together, and I knew they were thinking the same thing I was, namely: *Does that mean you're not going to tell on us?*

Ms. Weintraub sighed. "You geniuses may not have figured this out yet, but if word of this little . . . incident . . . leaks out, It's going to give more ammunition to the anti-alien crowd. A lot more. I have a greater interest in seeing Earth succeed in building a relationship with the rest of the galaxy than I do in seeing you three get your sorry butts fried. I can handle *that* myself. Believe me, you *will* pay for this . . . all three of you," she said significantly, directing her gaze at McNally.

"So what are we going to do?" I asked.

Bruce Coville

"We're going to go on just as if this had never happened. The class will be told that you and I had to step away for a while, Tim—which is pretty close to the truth."

"But who's going to take over the class?" asked McNally.

"You are," growled Ms. Weintraub, and even though her voice was tiny, it was clear that she meant business.

McNally groaned, and from the look on his face I realized that though he might be brave in battle and have nerves of steel, the idea of facing a classroom full of sixth graders had him downright terrified.

CHAPTER 15

[PLESKIT]
CHAOS IN THE CLASSROOM

We decided to station Tim and Ms. Weintraub in the top left drawer of Ms. Weintraub's desk. That way McNally could sit at the desk and, by leaning over, get advice from Ms. Weintraub on how to handle things.

If I had not been so upset, I would have laughed out loud at the look on my bodyguard's face when he tried to pick up the diminutive duo. I had not had a chance to explain the fact that they were still at their full weight. So when he wrapped one hand around Tim and the other around Ms. Weintraub, it was clear he was expecting them to weigh a few ounces each.

"Wait!" I cried.

He didn't wait. But when he tried to stand up it was as if his arms had been anchored to the floor.

"What the heck?" he growled.

"I tried to tell you—it is only their *size* that has been reduced. They have retained their original weight."

McNally made a face of disbelief, and tried again. After a bit of a struggle, he succeeded in lifting Ms. Weintraub.

"How much do you weigh, anyway?" he gasped.

Even I knew this was not a question you should ask a female Earthling.

"None of your business," Ms. Weintraub snapped. "Just get me in the desk like we planned. If you don't head outside soon to take my place, they're going to send someone in to find out what's keeping me."

McNally put Tim in the drawer, too. "Do not worry," I said peering in at the two tiny people. "You will be back to normal in just a few hours."

"It's those few hours that I'm worried about," muttered Ms. Weintraub.

Tim said nothing, but he looked miserable. I did not blame him. I had to go outside with McNally, of course;

I Shrank My Teacher

for him to leave the room without me would have been a major violation of his duty. But this meant Tim was going to be left alone with Ms. Weintraub.

I was sure she had plenty to say to him.

And I was glad I wasn't going to be around to hear it.

The playground wasn't too bad, because there were two other teachers on duty, so McNally did not really have to handle things. But when we got back to the classroom it soon became clear that my bodyguard was not born to be a teacher.

The kids, sensing this, were like *gnucks* who have scented blood. You could tell a feeding frenzy was building.

It was not that McNally could not have handled any one, or even two or three of them, individually. But they sensed that he couldn't handle the group. Even worse, they sensed that he did not want to go for outside help. So it was McNally against the rest of them, and they knew it.

Jordan got things started, which should be no surprise. When McNally announced that he was going to be handling the class until Ms. Weintraub returned,

Jordan said, "Are you a certified teacher?"

"I'm a certified butt-whupper," said McNally. "That ought to do for now."

From where I was sitting, I could hear a faint sound from the desk. I'm pretty sure it was Ms. Weintraub, trying to get McNally's attention.

Whatever the reason, he leaned toward the drawer.

When he sat up again, he said, "All right, it's time for the math test."

A chorus of groans filled the room. But this was a good move on Ms. Weintraub's part. McNally didn't actually have to teach to do this—just hand out the test and keep the class in line. Other than an astonishing number of pencil drops, and an occasional epidemic of coughing, it seemed to go fairly well.

Unfortunately, the test was not something he could make us do all afternoon. After about forty minutes even the slowest of the kids was done, and the class was getting restless.

So we had to move on to science.

The current unit had to do with simple tools. (Really simple, as far as I was concerned, since I had learned this stuff shortly after leaving the egg.)

I Shrank My Teacher

The lesson for the day was on levers. We were supposed to make our levers with rulers, which most of us already had of course, and a small block from the science kit that went underneath the ruler to use as a fulcrum.

Chris Mellblom and Misty Longacres passed out the fulcrums. They hadn't even finished when Jordan placed his ruler atop the fulcrum, put an eraser shaped like a hamburger on the lower end, then smashed his fist against the raised end. "Bombs away!" he cried.

The eraser sailed across the room, smacking Michael Wu in the head.

Michael sent it flying back toward Jordan.

Within moments the air was thick with unidentified flying objects.

I looked to see what McNally was going to do about the situation. His head was bent close to the desk drawer, and I could tell he was desperately trying to get advice from Ms. Weintraub on how to regain control of the class. But just as he stood up, there was a knock at the door.

Before anyone could answer, it swung open.

I heard a final clatter as the erasers, small pencil

sharpeners, blobs of chewed-up paper, and other items that had been flying about the room made their final landing. Everyone, including me, immediately tried to look innocent.

I suspect I did not succeed. Though I had not been participating in the catapult game, I still had plenty to feel guilty about.

Especially when I saw who was standing at the door.

CHAPTER 16

[T I M]

THE BOTTOM DROPS OUT

Being stuck in a desk drawer with a teacher that you have just shrunk is not a pleasant thing. Ms. Weintraub may be nice, and very pretty, but she is no softie.

"Sit down, Tim," she said when McNally first deposited us there. Her voice was hard and cold.

I sat on the edge of a pack of flash cards.

She began pacing back and forth in front of me (something she could do only because her drawer was a lot neater than any of mine have ever been) muttering angrily to herself. I had never seen her so upset. Finally she stopped and said, "What in heaven's name were you two thinking of to come up with a plan like this?"

"Desperate times require desperate measures," I said glumly, repeating a quote she had taught us in social studies.

"What desperate times?"

"The times of living with Jordan."

She sighed. "Look, Tim—I know Jordan bothers you. Frankly, he bothers me. But that's no excuse for this kind of stunt."

I hung my head. Then I started to cry. I didn't mean to. I didn't want to. It just came out. "You don't know what it's like," I sobbed.

Ms. Weintraub looked at me in astonishment.

"No," she whispered after a long time. "No, I don't."

Neither of us said anything for a while. She had one of those small packets of tissues in her drawer. She tore a corner off one and handed it to me. I wiped my face. Tears and snot. How charming.

Ms. Weintraub started to say something, stopped, started again. But before she could get out more than a few words we heard the class coming back in. She put a finger to her lips. I nodded.

I Shrank My Teacher

Listening to McNally try to handle the class would have been pretty hilarious, if things weren't so tense.

Then, just when things were really getting out of control, we heard the room fall totally silent.

"What's going on?" asked Ms. Weintraub, whispering despite the fact that her voice was already so tiny.

"I don't know," I said. "I'll see if I can find out."

I tried to grab the edge of the desk drawer so I could haul myself up to look, but it was a half inch or so higher than I could reach. I figured with one good jump I might be able to snag it.

I had underestimated myself. Since my muscles had lost nothing except the emptiness that fills most molecules, they were exactly as strong as they had ever been. Fortunately, my weight was also exactly the same as it had been before I shrank—otherwise, that jump might have sent me straight through the ceiling! As it was, I jumped exactly as high as I would have when I was full size—in other words, somewhere between eight and ten inches straight up. (That's without a running start, of course; just a straight jump.) But since I was only two inches high, an eight-inch jump sent me to four times my height!

What made it even worse was that since I had started from the desk drawer, at the peak of my jump I was about three feet above the floor. For a person who is about five feet (like I usually am), this would be like suddenly finding yourself ninety feet in the air—ninety feet up, and coming down fast.

Before I landed, I had a chance to see who had come into the room. Then I understood the gasp from the classroom.

Standing at the door were three people.

The first was a short man who looked vaguely familiar.

The second was the school principal, Mr. Grand.

The third was the dreaded Ms. Buttsman.

They did not look happy.

I saw all this in the briefest flash. Then I dropped back into the desk drawer.

The thing was, when I hit the bottom of the drawer, it was with the full force of my hundred and seven pounds.

Desk drawers are not constructed to survive having a two-inch object that weighs over a hundred pounds dropped into them. So when I hit the bottom of the drawer, I crashed right through it and kept on going.

And where was it I went?

Straight into the trash can that McNally had left underneath the drawer.

Ms. Weintraub came with me, of course, since I had pretty much ripped the bottom out of the drawer.

We plunged through layers of paper and trash, which helped cushion our fall and soften the noise of our landing. The other thing that saved us from disaster was that our bones and muscles, squeezed down to such a small size, were super dense and super strong.

Even so, the impact stunned us. After all, we hit with the full force of our regular weight. I can remember gazing around groggily at the crumpled papers that loomed over me like huge white boulders. My left foot was embedded in a wad of gum. A nearby apple core, a head taller than me, nearly overwhelmed me with its sweet smell.

"Help!" I called. "Help, someone!"

Despite the strength of my lungs, my vocal cords were tiny, and I couldn't get much volume.

And the layers of paper above me, blocking out

my view of the classroom, further muffled my voice.

Which was just as well, as it turned out. I was still squeaking for help when Ms. Weintraub put her hand on my shoulder and hissed, "Shhh! *Listen!*"

CHAPTER 17

[PLESKIT]
MR. TOMMAKKIO

When I saw Ms. Buttsman walk through the door of our classroom, I thought I was going to go into *kleptra*. What was she doing here? And what report would she make to the Fatherly One when she discovered what had been going on?

Even in my terror, I was distracted by a sound from Ms. Weintraub's desk. Because I was so aware of Tim and Ms. Weintraub being in the drawer, I turned in that direction at once. I heard another sound, a slight metallic *thunk*, as if McNally had accidentally kicked the trash can. But I saw nothing. So I turned my attention back to the door.

Mr. Grand's face was tight, grim, unamused. "Where is Ms. Weintraub?" he asked, looking directly at McNally.

"She . . . ah . . . well, that is . . . Tim had a slight . . . accident! Nothing serious, but it required immediate attention. I told her I would cover the class while she took Tim to get it taken care of."

"I'm not sure that was the *proper* way to deal with such a situation," said Ms. Buttsman.

"Well, it seemed like the *human* thing to do," replied McNally tartly. He glanced down at the drawer where Tim and Ms. Weintraub were hiding. He was good at controlling his facial expressions, so probably no one else saw what I did—a flash of terror and disbelief.

I felt my *clinkus* tighten in fear. What was going on now?

"I've brought some people to observe the class," said Mr. Grand. He turned to the room. "This is Ms. Kathryn Buttsman, who is the new protocol officer our government has assigned to the alien embassy. And this"—and here he gestured toward the short man who had come in with them—"is Mr. Tom Tommakkio, who is a federal school inspector."

"Don't mind us, Mr. McNally," said Ms. Buttsman with a terrible fake sweetness. "We'll just take a seat in the back of the room."

"I wish I could stay," said Mr. Grand. "Unfortunately, I have a pressing meeting. Mr. McNally, please tell Ms. Weintraub I'll want a report on whatever accident young Tompkins had."

"I'll be sure to give her the message," said McNally.

Mr. Grand nodded and left the room. Ms. Buttsman and Mr. Tommakkio headed for the back to take their seats.

The good news was that the arrival of the adults settled the class down some. The bad news was that poor McNally looked truly terrified. He waited until Ms. Buttsman and Mr. Tommakkio were seated, then cleared his throat and said, "We were just doing an experiment regarding . . . uh . . ."

I took advantage of his hesitation. "Regarding trajectories," I said loudly.

McNally looked at me in surprise. I could see relief in his eyes as he said quickly, "That's correct, Pleskit! Would you care to demonstrate?"

I had jumped in like that for two reasons. The first was that I knew the Fatherly One would be very unimpressed if Ms. Buttsman told him I was studying something as simple as the lever. The second was that poor McNally looked so terrified I felt I had to help him out—especially since it was my fault he was in this situation to begin with.

I joined him at the front desk. Looking out at the class, and especially toward Ms. Buttsman, I said, "The science of calculating trajectories is very interesting. By considering the angle, the length of both sides of the lever, the height of the fulcrum, the weight of the payload, and the force applied to send the payload flying, you can calculate the landing spot with great accuracy. That was what we were doing when you came in, O Honored Guests, which was why there was so much debris flying through the air. Allow me to demonstrate."

Going to the board, I drew an example of a lever, and quickly worked out some basic mathematics. Then I went to the desk and said, "Let us test my calculations, which were designed to send an object flying from the desk to the clock."

Putting a ruler on a wooden triangle, I picked up a red game piece called a checker and placed it on one end. "The trick," I said, positioning my hand above the other end of the ruler, "is to make sure I apply the correct amount of force."

Slamming my hand down, I sent the checker flying through the air. It struck the exact center of the clock.

The class broke into cheers. Ms. Buttsman smiled and gave me a tight little nod.

"Perhaps we should try one more," I said. "Let me make some notes."

I grabbed a piece of paper. But instead of equations, I scribbled, "Where are Ms. Weintraub and Tim?"

I slid the paper to McNally.

He looked at it. Out loud, he said, "Let's change those numbers just a bit, Pleskit." But on the paper he wrote, "I think they fell in the trash can!"

I barely managed not to yelp. Instead I stared at the paper for a minute, as if thinking about it, then said, "That's a tricky one, Mr. McNally. If I am going to do it, we'll have to retrieve the notes I made earlier."

McNally looked puzzled.

"The ones I threw in the wastepaper basket!" I said urgently.

"Oh, right!" said McNally. "You start the calculations, Pleskit. I'll get the old notes for you."

The class was looking pretty puzzled.

"Mr. McNally has challenged me to calculate a trajectory for landing this . . ."

"Peach," said McNally, grabbing the nearest thing he could find on Ms. Weintraub's desk.

"This . . . peach," I agreed, taking it from him, "into Ms. Buttsman's lap. Linnsy, would you measure the distance from the desk to Ms. Buttsman while I start the calculations?" Grabbing the container that had held the science materials, I added, "And would you give her this to catch it in, Jordan?"

Jordan scowled, but clearly did not want to create a scene in front of the visitors. He and Linnsy walked to the front of the room. Jordan took the container, while Linnsy grabbed a tape measure. I turned to the board and pretended I was trying to work out the calculations. I had already figured out the problem in my head, of course. But I wanted to give McNally time to get Tim and Ms. Weintraub out of the wastepaper basket.

"I can't find them . . ." he muttered.

Finally he just tipped the can on its side—which wasn't easy, given that there was over two hundred pounds of living mass at the bottom.

"Ah, here they are!" I said, grabbing the first piece of paper that came to hand. I was relieved to see Tim and Ms. Weintraub scoot out of the basket and hide under the desk.

Quickly I finished my calculations. "Ready, Ms. Buttsman?" I called, placing the peach on the ruler.

"Really, Pleskit," she said, standing up. "I think this is a bad idea. Mr. Tommakkio, I think we should go now, and come back when the real teacher is here. But before we leave the school, I want to register a complaint at the head office. This is simply not proper."

"Sit down, Ms. Buttsman," said Mr. Tommakkio quietly.

"No, really," said Ms. Buttsman. "It is time for us to leave."

Mr. Tommakkio reached into his coat. When he withdrew his hand, he was holding a large purple ray gun.

"I said, sit down."

Ms. Buttsman sat.

CHAPTER 18

[TIM]
UNDER THE DESK

Ms. Weintraub and I crouched in the trash can listening to what happened when the visitors came in. When she heard Mr. Grand introduce Ms. Buttsman and the government Inspector, she groaned. "That's it! My career is over."

"It's not your fault," I said. "We'll explain what happened."

Of course, once we had done that, it would probably be our lives instead of Ms. Weintraub's career that came to an end. But I didn't say that out loud.

While Pleskit and McNally tried to bluff their way through the lesson, I scraped the gum off my foot.

Then I explored the bottom of the trash can—which wasn't easy, since I couldn't get all the gum off, and it kept sticking to things. Also, given our height, it was like trying to explore a round room that was more than twenty feet across, and covered from one side to the other with pieces of trash the size of sofas.

We considered trying to knock the can over—with our combined weight and strength I think we could have managed it. But that would have ruined any chance we had of keeping our condition secret.

At one point I stumbled into a heap of something like dirty sawdust. After a second I realized it was the grindings from the pencil sharpener that someone had dumped into the can. I managed to smear black stuff all over my hands trying to get out of that. Before long I had it on my clothes and my face, too.

Then McNally tipped the can over for us.

"Tim!" whispered Ms. Weintraub. "Come on—now's our chance!"

Fighting my way through the wads of paper, I followed her out of the can. Hoping we wouldn't be seen, we scurried under her desk, then climbed up onto one of the chair legs. I was a little surprised at how easily Ms. Weintraub made the climb—more easily than I was able to—until I remembered that she was a gymnast.

We had just settled on the crossbar under the chair, which was a little like sitting on a square tree branch, when we heard a cry of outrage from Ms. Buttsman, then a general hubbub from the classroom, then an unfamiliar voice bellow, "No one move!"

Ms. Weintraub clutched my arm. "What's going on *now?*"

"I don't know. I'll find out."

Scrambling down from the chair, I crawled to the edge of the desk.

I didn't need to worry about being seen. Everyone's attention was riveted to the back of the room, where Mr. Tommakkio was pointing something that looked like a big, goofy water pistol at Ms. Buttsman. Suddenly I realized where I had seen Mr. Tommakkio before: He was the guy who had been watching me in the park last Saturday, when I left the embassy after our trip to the mall.

"No one is leaving this place until the teacher returns with Tim Tompkins," said Mr. Tommakkio.

That sizzled my brain, I want to tell you. What did this guy want with *me?*

Fortunately, I was going to be very hard to find at the moment.

Unfortunately, I had no idea when the compacting ray was going to wear off, and I would shoot back to full size. Suddenly I realized that I didn't want to be under the desk when that happened.

"If you will all sit quietly, no one will get hurt," said Mr. Tommakkio. "Mr. McNally, how much longer do you think it will be before the teacher returns with young Tompkins?"

"I honestly have no idea," said McNally.

Tommakkio looked around at the classroom. "I'm sure you all have work to do. Take out something and get busy. Remain quiet. Pleskit, return to your seat. Mr. McNally, deposit your gun on the desk and do the same."

I felt a hand on my shoulder and barely kept myself from jumping—which was just as well, since I probably would have smashed my head against the desk.

It was Ms. Weintraub, of course. (No one else was small enough to put their hand on my shoulder anyway!)

I Shrank My Teacher

"What are we going to do?" she whispered.

"Come on," I said. "I've got an idea!"

"It was your ideas that got us into this in the first place," said Ms. Weintraub bitterly.

But she followed me anyway.

The trip to Pleskit's desk was not easy, since it was important that we not be seen. We darted out from under the side of Ms. Weintraub's desk and scurried behind a nearby book rack.

Dropping to my belly, I crawled to the edge and peered out at the room, which was filled with towering giants.

Luck was with us. Everyone was still staring at Mr. Tommakkio. Ms. Weintraub and I scooted to the far wall. This was a good place for us, because the shelf units had a space under them, about three inches high and six inches deep, where we could move without being seen.

"If we ever get out of this, I'm going to have a little talk with the janitor," muttered Ms. Weintraub as she pushed aside a dust bunny that came up to her shoulder.

Moving cautiously, we followed the wall until we

came to Pleskit's row. Getting over to his desk was a little trickier, because we were in the open for much of the time, but by hiding behind backpacks and book-bags, we managed it.

Now all I had to do was get his attention.

CHAPTER 19

[PLESKIT]
TIM'S BRAINSTORM

Mr. Tommakkio ordered McNally and me to return to our seats.

We did as he directed. Inside, I felt the coldness of *pizumpta*. And though McNally's face was expressionless, I could sense his fury and despair.

I went to my desk and took out some work. I bent over it, just as the others had. However, I suspect no one was *really* working. I certainly wasn't. Who could concentrate with this strange man holding us hostage?

Suddenly I felt something tugging at the leg of my jeans. Looking down, I barely kept myself from shouting.

It was tiny Tim!

He motioned for me to bend over so I could talk to him. I glanced toward the front of the room. Mr. Tommakkio had his ray gun in his hand and was glaring around. I moved my hand slightly, causing my pencil to fall to the floor. "Oops!" I said, and bent as if to pick it up.

"I've got an idea!" said Tim when I was close enough for him to speak into my ear.

"What is it?" I whispered.

"Let's use a catapult to knock Mr. Tommakkio out! You can calculate the trajectory, and we'll smack him right between the eyes."

"Are you crazy? I can't knock him out with a checker! We don't have a missile heavy enough to do anything more than slightly annoy him."

"Yes, we do."

"What?"

"Me! I'm only two inches tall, but I've still got my full weight! I'd knock him on his butt in an instant."

"And how am I going to send you flying there to begin with? I couldn't hit the ruler hard enough to lift you, much less send you flying through the air."

"Pleskit!" said Mr. Tommakkio sharply. "What are you doing?"

I Shrank My Teacher

"Just getting my pencil," I said, sitting up quickly.

A minute later I felt another tug at my leg. I looked down. Tim was gesturing frantically for me to talk to him again. I glanced at Mr. Tommakkio. His gaze continued to shift around the room, his eyes darting back and forth as if nothing could escape them.

"Ow!" I said. "Something bit me!"

I bent down again, as if to check my ankle.

"Change of plan," said Tim. "Set up the lever. I'll jump on the end, and send Ms. Weintraub flying. If I jump from the rung of your desk, it should give us enough force."

With excitement, I realized that this could work. Since he still had his full weight, Tim could provide the force needed. But the calculations were going to be difficult. I needed exact numbers, and I did not have them. I had to estimate the distance from my desk to the front of the room. And I was going to have to guess at both Tim's and Ms. Weintraub's weights. What if I made a mistake and sent our teacher splatting against the blackboard?

I felt another tug on my jeans.

I glanced down. Tim and Ms. Weintraub were standing

in the shelter of my backpack, which hid them from most people's sight. I started to bend over, but Tim shook his head—which was just as well, because I was already making Tommakkio suspicious. Tim pointed at Ms. Weintraub. Then he held up both hands and spread his fingers. He did this twelve times, then held up just two fingers. Then he spread his hands in a gesture that he later explained to me means, "Get it?"

I didn't get it. My puzzlement must have shown on my face, because he started again.

This time I got it. He was telling me that Ms. Weintraub weighed 122 pounds!

Next he pointed to himself and made the same set of gestures, only this time he held up both hands ten times, then held up seven fingers.

107 pounds.

Now I could do the calculations with much greater accuracy.

This left three problems. The first was the matter of the tool. Obviously we could not use one of the school's wooden rulers. With 122 pounds on one end, if Tim jumped onto the other end, it would simply snap in half.

I Shrank My Teacher

The second was getting Tim in position to make his jump. Since he weighed 107 pounds, I could not lift him. He was going to have to climb into position himself. I was not sure he would be able to do this. I liked Tim a lot, but I had already noticed that physical education was not his specialty.

The third problem was getting the catapult set up without attracting Tommakkio's attention. It would not take long, but it was going to be tricky.

The first problem was actually fairly easy to solve. In my desk I had a straight-edge measuring stick that I had brought from Hevi-Hevi. The material is low-grade by our standards. Even so, it can withstand an impact of several thousand pounds. It was also a little longer than a standard Earth ruler, which gave me more freedom in working out my calculations.

The second problem was trickier, but not impossible. My backpack was leaning against the desk, and I hoped Tim would be able to climb it to get himself into position. Of course, I also had to let him know *where* he was supposed to position himself.

I caught his eye—not hard, since he and Ms. Weintraub were watching me like *sparrziks*. Reaching under my desk, I tapped the spot I wanted him to leap from.

To my surprise, even though the rung of the desk was more than three times his height off the floor, he jumped up and grabbed it. I had forgotten that his muscles still had their full strength.

Now all I had to solve was the third problem—getting the catapult in place.

Alas, this one seemed impossible. My activity had already attracted Tommakkio's attention. He was glaring at me. His eyes, which did not turn away, had a hard look of hatred in them.

A familiar look.

Suddenly I realized who Tommakkio really was.

Cold fear twisted my *clinkus*.

CHAPTER 20

[TIM]

THE HUMAN BULLET

It was incredibly frustrating not to be able to talk to Pleskit. But if we tried to communicate too much, Tommakkio would be sure to realize something was going on. So I had to figure out on my own what was holding him up.

Well, not entirely on my own. When I muttered, "What's he waiting for?" Ms. Weintraub replied, "He needs some sort of distraction before he can set up the catapult."

I was sitting on the rung of the desk, exactly where Pleskit had indicated. Ms. Weintraub was standing below me, ready to take her place on the catapult. She had closed her eyes and seemed to be doing some sort of deep-breathing exercise. Also, she had her fingers crossed on both hands. Suddenly I realized that my idea was not entirely foolproof. I was expecting her to give an Olympic-level performance without any real practice!

Of course, she wasn't even going to be able to try unless Pleskit could set up that catapult.

I glanced around. No one had noticed us—not surprising, considering our size. Besides, even though everyone was supposed to be working, all attention was riveted on the front of the room. I dropped to the floor. The desk legs rising next to me looked like mighty tree trunks. Pleskit's backpack was like a huge canvas hill.

"I'll be right back," I said.

Jordan was sitting two rows over. Ducking, crawling, sprinting, hiding, I made my way to his desk. As I went, I picked up a pencil I had noticed on the floor. I was pleased to see that it was still sharp. It was nearly twice as long as me, and thicker than my leg, but since I still had my full strength, carrying it was no problem.

I scurried under Jordan's desk.

"Sorry, Jordan," I whispered. "I'm only doing this for the good of the class."

Then I jabbed him in the ankle as hard as I could.

Jordan howled and jumped up, clutching at his ankle.

"Sit down!" roared Tommakkio, pointing his ray gun at Jordan.

Jordan flung his hands into the air. "Something stung me! I think it was a bee!"

"I'm allergic to bees!" cried Tyrone Walker nervously.

"Me, too!" shouted Misty. "I could die from a bee sting!"

"Sit down!" bellowed Tommakkio. "All of you. *Now!*"

During the confusion I scurried, unnoticed, back to Pleskit's desk.

"That wasn't very nice," whispered Ms. Weintraub. But I noticed she was smiling.

Pleskit had put the catapult in place during the confusion.

I scrambled back into position on the desk rung.

Ms. Weintraub climbed onto the end of the lever.

I heard a little gasp. Rafaella Cruz, who sits across the aisle from Pleskit, had just seen us.

Ms. Weintraub put her finger to her lips in a sign to be silent. Rafaella, wide-eyed, nodded.

I tensed myself, waiting for Pleskit's signal. His

head—so big compared to me at this size that it looked like a weather balloon—appeared at the edge of the desk. He was frowning. "Not yet," he mouthed, and I knew he was waiting for Tommakkio, who had moved during the fuss, to get back in place.

Jordan was still complaining about his "sting." The kids who were nervous about bees were shifting their chairs.

Suddenly Pleskit shouted, "Now, Tim! *NOW!*"

I leaped from the desk rung, directly onto the raised end of the lever. The full force of my 107 pounds drove it straight to the floor.

Ms. Weintraub soared over my head—122 pounds of gymnastic ability packed into a living, two-inch-high projectile.

Then, to my horror, Tommakkio moved! Ms. Weintraub shot past him and struck the blackboard! I thought we were sunk. But she struck the board with her feet, bounced off it, did a perfect double flip, and slammed into the back of Tommakkio's head.

With a groan, he fell face forward on the desk.

The class burst into cheers.

McNally sprinted for the front of the room. In an

instant he had Tommakkio in an armlock. At the same time he kicked the purple ray gun and sent it skittering across the floor.

Ms. Weintraub, acknowledging the cheers of the class, was dancing along the edge of her desk, smiling and waving.

I couldn't see what happened next, but Pleskit told me about it afterward. Linnsy was the one who started it. She tore a piece of paper out of her notebook, wrote a big 10 on it, and held it up. Soon every kid in the room was holding up a "scorecard" and shouting, "Ten! Ten! Ten!"

We had one more surprise coming. When McNally pulled back Tommakkio's head, the movement loosened the intruder's mask. McNally pulled it off to reveal the furry face of . . . Mikta-makta-mookta!

Which was one reason Pleskit and I didn't get in nearly as much trouble for borrowing the Molecule Compactor as we had expected to. If Ms. Weintraub and I had not been shrunken when Mikta-makta-mookta fooled the Butt into bringing her into the classroom, she might have succeeded in her plan to kidnap Pleskit

and me. Her motive? Revenge, of course, for our thwart-
ing the plot she and her evil partner Harr-giss had been
hatching to ruin the peaceful alien mission.

Ms. Weintraub was still standing on her desk when
the compacting ray wore off. She was so surprised she
stumbled backward—which was odd, given her gymnastics skills. Fortunately, McNally—who had already
tied up Tommakkio/Mikta-makta-mookta—caught her.

I shot up at the same time, of course. Fortunately,
I was standing in the middle of the aisle, so I didn't
bump my head on anything.

Ms. Buttsman was so startled by our sudden
growth that she fainted. Unfortunately (for her) no
one caught her.

I noticed that McNally took just a moment longer to
set Ms. Weintraub down than he really should have. At
least, *I* thought he took too long. My mother has told
me it's none of my business.

She has also threatened me with permanent
grounding and several other forms of doom and
destruction if I ever, *ever*, EVER do anything like this
again. But aside from the fact that she is incredibly

upset that I have been in so much danger twice since the beginning of school, I think she was pretty pleased with my part in capturing Mikta-makta-mookta.

One other thing happened as a result of all this. The next day, and against my advice, Pleskit wore his "Victory Outfit" to school. That was the purple-and-green one-piece with sparkling spirals all over it.

Do you know what happened when he walked through the door wearing it?

Everyone shouted, "Hey, that's cool!"

I swear, I wanted to scream.

CHAPTER 21

[PLESKIT]
A LETTER HOME

**FROM: Pleskit Meenom, on the slightly cool
Planet Earth
TO: Maktel Geebrit, on the beloved Planet
Hevi-Hevi**

Dear Maktel:

Well, there you have it—the story of how
I survived my second major crisis on Earth.

I wonder if life here will ever get any easier.

At least I didn't get kicked off the planet.
So it still beats Geembol Seven.

The Fatherly One was very angry about
my borrowing his Molecule Compactor, of

course. But he was also chagrined because it was his "wonderful new employee," Ms. Buttsman, who let Mikta-makta-mookta into the classroom. So things sort of balanced out in that regard.

Much as I would like to let Ms. Buttsman take all the blame, it wasn't really her fault. Because Mikta-makta-mookta had worked in the embassy, she knew our rules and procedures. So she had been able to fake documents presenting herself as a school inspector that met all the security standards, even passed the electronic scanning test. Given all that, Ms. Buttsman had no reason not to believe "Mr. Tommakkio" was real.

Even so, I could tell she was plenty embarrassed about her part in the whole sorry mess.

Speaking of embassy staff—here's a news flash: Yesterday the Fatherly One informed us that his new assistant, Beezle Whompis, will arrive in less than a week.

Please join me in hoping that he/she/it

will be someone/something I can get along with. I have been told only that this being is (a) extremely efficient, (b) has the highest possible rating for loyalty and dedication (headquarters owes *that* to the Fatherly One, after assigning him the traitorous Mikta-makta-mookta the first time around), and (c) is categorized as an "alternate life-form." That should be interesting. I wonder how Tim will react when he meets a being as weird (by Earth standards) as this one is bound to be.

Oh, well. I can't worry about that now. I have enough troubles already.

On the other hand, things could be worse. At least some of the kids think I'm "cool" now. And we no longer have to worry about Mikta-makta-mookta being on the loose.

I have to get ready for school, so I'll sign off. I hope, *hope*, HOPE you can come visit sometime soon.

Until then—*Fremmix Bleeblom!*

Your chilly pal,

Pleskit

SPECIAL BONUS:

On the following pages you will find Part Two of "Disaster on Geembol Seven"—the story of what happened to Pleskit on the last planet where he lived before coming to Earth.

This story will be told in six thrilling installments, one included at the end of each of the first six books in the Sixth-Grade Alien series.

Look for the next installment at the end of Book Three, *Missing—One Brain*!

DISASTER ON GEEMBOL SEVEN

PART TWO:
TO LISTEN IS A CRIME

FROM: Pleskit Meenom, on Planet Earth
TO: Maktel Geebrit, on Planet Hevi-Hevi
Dear Maktel:

Okay, I am ready to tell you a little more about what happened on Geembol Seven.

Just to remind you: The Fatherly One and I went into the city on the night of the moondance. Separated from the Fatherly One, I spotted a six-eyed boy who seemed to need help. I followed him to the waterside, where we sat under one of the huge old docks to talk. But when I leaned against one of the pilings, it opened up and a cold hand pulled me inside.

Here is what happened next:

"Shhh!" hissed a voice close to my ear. "Stay quiet, and I won't hurt you. Make a sound, and it may be your last!"

The voice was wet and bubbly, as if whomever it belonged to were speaking through a layer of water. I stayed quiet. The boy I had followed slipped through the opening as well. Once he was inside, it slid shut.

The darkness was complete—as was my terror.

My *sphen-gnut-ksher* began to spark.

"Don't try using that thing on me," snarled my captor. "I'm shielded against it."

As he still had his hand over my mouth, I could not explain that I did not have complete control over the *sphen-gnut-ksher's* protective eruptions, that they happened instinctively if my body felt I was in enough danger to warrant them.

By the intermittent light of my own sparks I could see the face of the six-eyed boy.

He looked as sad as ever. But now his face showed terror, too.

"Let him go, Balteeri," said the boy suddenly. "We shouldn't have done this. It was a mistake."

"It's too late to turn back now, Derrvan."

Before the boy could respond, the ground began to sink beneath us. I felt a new jolt of fear. Were we caught in some kind of earthquake? My fear subsided a little when the smoothness of our descent made me realize that the inside of the piling was actually a kind of elevator. Not that I stopped being afraid altogether. After all, I was still a captive, being dragged below the surface of a planet that I had only been living on for a few days.

The elevator stopped and I was pulled backward into a large sandcave. Blue glowballs mounted on posts provided dim illumination. Pulsing green things clung to the ceiling. Their long tentacles dangled beneath them, writhing and twisting.

Balteeri released his grip on me. He didn't need to tell me not to run. The cave was small; there was no place to escape to, no tunnels to hide myself in.

I turned to face him. To my surprise and horror, he was not a completely organic being, but rather a strange mix of mechanical and living parts. He had four arms—three mechanical, one made of flesh. The mechanical arms each had a tool where the hand or tentacles would normally have been. One of his eyes was real, the other clearly mechanical. His writhing metallic tail was as thick as my arm. Such constructs have been forbidden since the Delfiner War, of course. So where could he have come from?

Though the Fatherly One has been trying to teach me to hide my emotions (an important skill for a diplomatic trader), my training failed me then.

"Ah," said Balteeri when he saw the look on my face. "You are not used to seeing illegal beings. At least, you think you are not

used to it. From my point of view, *you* are illegal, young Hevi-Hevian. What do you think of that?"

I didn't know what to think, and I said so.

My captor laughed, an odd, bubbling kind of sound. "No, you wouldn't, would you? Children are rarely taught the sins of their parents. Only the stories of glory get passed along."

"What do you want of me? I am here as part of a diplomatic mission, and as such I have immunity. If I am harmed, there will be grave consequences."

I spoke these words firmly, which was something I was taught almost from the day I had emerged from my egg.

My captor laughed again. "Your being brought down here *is* a grave consequence—a consequence of other actions, taken by other beings. Everything has consequences, young Hevi-Hevian, and they spread through time like ripples through the sea. As to the consequences for myself—well, the greater one's desperation, the greater one's anger, the greater the injustice one has suffered, the less one cares for threats like that."

"Enough, Balteeri," said the boy who had gotten me into this. "We didn't bring him here to terrorize him."

The construct blinked and nodded. "Forgive me, Derrvan. Sometimes I grant my anger more power over my emotions than is wise. You are correct."

One of the tentacled beasts clinging to the cave's ceiling fell to the floor. It landed with a soggy *plop* and began squirming in our direction. Derrvan stepped aside nervously. But Balteeri simply pursed his lips and emitted a high-pitched squeal. The creature quivered and pulled its tentacles in so that it looked like nothing more than a blob of green jelly.

I turned to Derrvan. "Why bother with all this, with dragging me down here, with scaring me so much, if all you want is my help? That was why I followed you—so I could help you."

"Would you have agreed to come with me

if you knew about my companion?" asked the boy.

I glanced at Balteeri nervously but did not answer.

Derrvan narrowed his six eyes and asked intently, "Would you have agreed to listen to my story if you knew that listening to it could make you a criminal?"

The fear this comment gave me was different from the physical fear that struck when I was pulled into the piling. This was a small, tight, cold fear, centered in my *clinkus*.

"How can simply listening to a story be a crime?" I asked.

"How can simply existing be a crime?" replied Balteeri bitterly.

For that I had no answer.

"Will you listen to this story?" asked Derrvan. "I repeat: For you to listen to it here on Geembol Seven is a crime. I will not force you—"

Balteeri made a growling sound, but Derrvan waved him to silence.

"If you decline, we will return you to the

surface, and you will suffer nothing more than unfulfilled curiosity, and perhaps, sometimes late at night, a slight twinge of guilt. To listen is a crime, but in listening you open yourself to the chance to right an ancient wrong so foul that the memory of it cries to the stars."

"Why me?" I asked, partly because I was baffled by his words, but even more to gain time, time to make a decision, time to try to understand.

"Because it is easier to speak truth to youth," said Balteeri. "Those who have achieved adulthood are often so sure they know what is real that they cannot hear truth even when it is shouting in their ears, cannot see what is true even when it slaps them on the face and cries, 'Look at me! See me! Listen to my story!'"

I nodded. "If I do listen to your story . . . then what?"

"Then you will also be faced with another choice," said Derrvan. "The choice of whether you will help us or not. I warn you now, helping us will be an even greater crime than listening to our story."

"But what happened was a great crime, too," said Balteeri darkly. "Not a violation of law, perhaps, but a crime against decency."

I looked at the two of them—Derrvan, so young and frightened, his six eyes brimming with sorrow, with need, with hope, with fear (you can express a lot with six eyes); Balteeri so angry and yet so righteous—and I thought of something the Fatherly One has often said to me: "We trade in strange and precious things gathered from all across the galaxy. Yet of all the things that I have seen, nothing is more strange and precious than the Truth. Grab it when you can."

"Tell me your story," I said.

Before Derrvan could speak, something burst through the wall of the cave.

To be continued . . .

A GLOSSARY OF ALIEN TERMS USED BY PLESKIT

Following is a list of Hevi-Hevian words and phrases used by Pleskit in Books One and Two of Sixth-Grade Alien. The numerals after the definitions indicate the book and chapter where the term was first used— for example (I:4) means the term first appeared in Book One, Chapter Four.

Though we are only giving the spelling of the words here, in actual usage many of them would be accompanied by smells or body sounds.

CLINKUS: an internal organ connecting the breathing and the digestive systems (I:4).

FEBRIL GNURXIS: a sweet, nutritious breakfast cereal (I:4).

FEEBRIX: an essential part of the reproductive process on Hevi-Hevi (II:10).

FIN-POK: a sweet snack, made from grain, pollen, and living honey (plural: finnikle-pokta) (I:17).

FINUSSHER: release bodily wastes (I:6).

FLINKEL: a large creature, something like a cat only covered with stiff green scales; known for its ferocity (I:2).

FREMMIX BLEEBLOM: traditional Hevi-Hevi words of farewell; loose translation "May the stars sit on your shoulder" (I:2).

GEZUP-GEZOP: basically, "If that's what you really want!" Considered slightly vulgar, and always used in an angry or sarcastic way (I:4).

GIB-STIKKLE: unusual, strange, goofy (I:26).

GNERF: an annoying, insectlike creature (ten legs, hard green exoskeleton) that inhabits cargo ships. Used as a term of insult, as in "you little gnerf" (I:21).

GNUCKS: small, predatory creatures, something like lizards with wings; known for the vicious way they attack anything that has the scent of blood on it. They travel in packs and can strip a large animal to its bones in a matter of minutes (I:6).

GULZEEMIA: legendary lost city; capital of the first Hevi-Hevian empire (I:18).

I Shrank My Teacher

KLEPTRA: a state of mental and physical shutdown created by excess stress, as in "By the time the exam was over I thought I would go into *kleptra*" (I:8).

KLIMPLED: overwhelmed by excess stimuli; as in "The amusement park was so crowded, smelly, and noisy that Pingdl Foosian began to feel *klimpled*" (I:7).

KLING-GHAT: a formal robe, used for special occasions. Usually, but not always, decorated with shifting symbols that tell important myth-stories (I:4).

KLING-KPHUT: a temporary state of unconsciousness, usually quite blissful. Though normally attained by meditation, a blast from a *sphen-gnut-ksher* can also throw someone into *kling-kphut* (I:10).

MEETUMLICHT: binding to one's honor (I:2).

PINGLIES: large, four-eyed amphibians that roam the subtropical wampfields of Hevi-Hevi; the size of cows (but built like frogs) they tend to travel in packs (I:8).

PIZUMPTA: a special state of dread created by social blunders and causing the internal organs to go cold; a sensitive Hevi-Hevian in an advanced state of *pizumpta* may need to be hospitalized (I:8).

PLINKTUM: an internal organ, part of the circulatory system (I:12).

PLONKUS: a blubbery creature found in the northern ponds of Hevi-Hevi. Known for extreme gluttony; given enough food, a *plonkus* will eat until it cannot move. In extreme cases they have been known to explode (I:12).

SKEEZPUL: a word too naughty to translate! (I:19).

SKIGPOO: bad, suspicious, slimy, or rotten (I:18).

SKAKKA: large, slow herd animal. Extremely tasty when cooked in the proper fashion but deadly poisonous if not prepared correctly (I:6).

SPARTZIKS: trained hunting lizards (II:19).

SPHEN-GNUT-KSHER: the stalk and knob that grow from the top of a Hevi-Hevian's head; used to gather both information and energy, and also for self-protection (I:4).

SPLORK: erupt with anger; a rare action, considered inappropriate to a civilized being in all but the most extreme circumstances (II:9).

SPLURGIS: a sweet delicacy, taken from the inside of large pods that grow deep under the wampfields (II:3).

SPRINDLE A GLIXXIT: a slightly vulgar expression for extreme emotional reaction; literally "fart so hard it breaks the chair" (II:10).

WHIZZORIA: place where you *finussher*; self-cleaning (I:16).